"Hailey. Listen to me." His voice shook as he spoke. "You can't travel to the Middle East right now."

"But—"

"It's not safe. Your brother didn't want you in danger."

She heard the plea in his voice. "But mission work is dangerous. Clay knew that. I know it, too."

"I don't care how prepared you think you are, you can't go there alone."

She touched his shoulder, surprised at the tension she felt under her hand. "I won't be alone. I'll have others with me. And, of course, I'll have God."

His shocked gaze locked with hers. "The Lord can't protect you from roadside bombs."

Looking into Wolf's angry expression, Hailey knew words wouldn't get through to him now. But maybe a firsthand account would.

"Come to church with me this afternoon," she said. "A couple who are permanently based in the Middle East are visiting," she explained.

"You're not going to listen to another word I say unless I agree to this, are you?"

"Nope."

"You are one hard-headed woman, Hailey O'Brien." H⋯⋯⋯⋯⋯on.

"So I've bee⋯⋯

Books by Renee Ryan

Love Inspired

Homecoming Hero

Love Inspired Historical

*The Marshal Takes a Bride
*Hannah's Beau
Heartland Wedding
*Loving Bella

*Charity House

RENEE RYAN

grew up in a small Florida beach town. To entertain herself during countless hours of "lying out" she read all the classics. It wasn't until the summer between her sophomore and junior years at Florida State University that she read her first romance novel. Hooked from page one, she spent hours consuming one book after another while working on the best (and last!) tan of her life.

Two years later, armed with a degree in economics and religion, she explored various career opportunities, including stints at a Florida theme park, a modeling agency and a cosmetics conglomerate. She moved on to teach high school economics, American government and Latin while coaching award-winning cheerleading teams. Several years later, with an eclectic cast of characters swimming around in her head, she began seriously pursuing a writing career.

She lives an action-packed life in Lincoln, Nebraska, with her supportive husband, lovely teenage daughter and two ornery cats who hate each other.

Homecoming Hero
Renee Ryan

Steeple
Hill®

Published by Steeple Hill Books™

Homecoming Hero
Renee Ryan

STEEPLE HILL BOOKS

Steeple
Hill®

Recycling programs
for this product may
not exist in your area.

ISBN-13: 978-0-373-87617-4

HOMECOMING HERO

Copyright © 2010 by Renee Halverson

www.SteepleHill.com

Printed in U.S.A.

Come to me, all you who are weary and burdened,
and I will give you rest.

—*Matthew* 11:28

To First Lieutenant Erik J. Anthes. I'm humbled
by your continued dedication to our country.
Thank you for your service, my friend.
May God keep you safe and in His arms always.

Chapter One

U.S. Army Captain Ty Wolfson stared at his friend's childhood home in stunned silence. He'd been so focused on getting off post he hadn't considered what he might find once he arrived in Savannah. The possibility that he'd be standing in front of a two-hundred-year-old house in the heart of the historic district hadn't crossed his mind.

Not once.

But here Wolf stood, confronting generations of tradition, wrapped up neatly in what the historical marker deemed O'Brien House.

As he read the story of the O'Brien family history, guilt twisted painfully in his gut. It should be Clay preparing to climb up these steps. Not Wolf. Not like this, under these terrible circumstances.

And yet...he *would* walk inside that house. To fulfill the promise he'd made to Clay on that Iraqi roadside.

Determined to accomplish the difficult task before him, Wolf started forward, but a jolt of sorrow knifed through him. The feeling was so strong, so visceral he had to stop and swallow several times to get the emotion under control.

Breathing hard, he lowered his gaze to the grainy photograph he'd kept with him for the last six months. The sight of Clay's little sister grinning back at him made Wolf's heartbeat quicken with anxiety.

Dressed in a traditional graduation gown with the requisite mortarboard scrunched on top of her head, Hailey O'Brien looked far too young, and far too innocent to have set such a dangerous course for her life.

Whatever it took, Wolf would stop her. He owed that much to Clay. And the friendship they'd shared in Iraq.

Blinking the grit out of his eyes, he stuffed the photograph back in his pocket and studied Clay's childhood home a moment longer. He knew he was stalling, but he needed a chance to take it all in.

The three-story brick mansion filled an entire city block. Each floor boasted rows of tall, double-glass doorways leading onto cast-iron balconies. A fence in the same ornate design ran along the perimeter of the manicured lawn, encircling tall trees and large bushes that reached halfway to the second floor.

With his gaze tracking the adjacent streets, Wolf experienced a sense of claustrophobia. There were too many trees in this part of town and the houses were too close together. He'd lived too long in the desert not to feel pinned in now.

Shivering, he blew into his cupped palms. The temperature had dropped to a sharp, bitter cold that turned his breath to frost. Clay had prepared him for the heat, with his constant griping about the Savannah humidity. But he'd said nothing about this bone-rattling cold that made Wolf's leg ache more than usual.

A light mist swirled in the gray, depressing air. The perfect accompaniment for all the regrets he harbored in his heart. Duty was all he had left. Duty and this one goal, the fulfillment of his promise to a fallen friend.

"Might as well get this over with," he muttered.

Gritting his teeth, Wolf set out across the street. He hid the pain in his left leg behind an even gait and stone-cold determination.

After three sharp raps of the ornate knocker the door swung open. Wolf jerked in surprise. With her dark hair, big green eyes and curvy figure, Hailey O'Brien was not the teenager he'd prepared for in his mind. She was a woman—a throat-clogging, heart-stopping, *beautiful* woman.

He knew he was staring. How could he not? Clay's sister was nothing like the fuzzy graduation picture her brother had kept on the dash of their Humvee and Wolf now had in his pocket.

Wolf tried to speak. Even managed to open his mouth, but memories got in the way and he pressed his lips tightly together. His head filled with contrasting images of Clay kicking around a soccer ball with some local kids outside the forward operating base. Clay blinking up at him on the Iraqi roadside as he was bleeding out.

Clay issuing the request that had brought Wolf to this house today…

You gotta keep Hailey out of the Sandpit, Wolf-man. No mission work. Not here. Promise me you'll stop her.

Wolf hadn't hesitated in his response. *I won't let you down.*

The memory of his own words pushed Wolf into action. "Are you Hailey O'Brien?"

She nodded. Slowly. And it finally registered that she'd been standing there speechless, just like him.

Even now, she simply stared at him with her beautiful, unguarded, attentive eyes. Waiting. Watching.

"I..." Wolf cleared his throat. "I was a friend of your brother's."

Instant pain filled her gaze and the wall went up. Wolf hadn't expected that.

"You knew Clay?" she asked at last, her voice deeper and throatier than he'd expected.

"I did. He asked me to—" Wolf cut off his words midsentence, realizing he couldn't blurt out why he was here without some sort of buildup. "That is, I was with him when he died." Which wasn't what he'd meant to say, either.

She blinked. "You were?"

"Yes."

She blinked again. And then...

One lone tear slid down her cheek.

Great beginning, Wolf, you made the poor woman cry.

With concentrated effort, he softened his voice. "My name is Ty. Ty Wolfson."

"Wolf." Her shoulders snapped back. "Yes, of course. I should have...expected this."

"You know me?"

She nodded. "My brother mentioned you in his e-mails."

Wolf didn't know what to do with that information, so he redirected the conversation. "Is this a bad time?" He shifted his gaze, only just noticing the purse strapped around her shoulder and the coat slung over her arm. "You look ready to go out."

"Oh. I... No." She drew her bottom lip between her teeth. "I mean, I am heading out, but it can wait."

Okay, good. He had her attention again. Now, if he

could get his tongue to work properly he might be able to finish what he'd come here to do. Then he could return to his temporary housing on post and give in to his exhaustion. The forty-eight-hour journey out of Iraq was catching up with him.

"What I have to say won't take long," he promised. Not if he could help it.

"Oh. *Oh.* I'm so sorry. I'm being rude, making you stand out there in the cold." She gave him a quick, tense smile. "Please. Come in. I don't know what I was thinking."

Wolf heard the genuine remorse in her words, saw the guilt in her eyes and felt bad for upsetting her. "No worries. I didn't give you any warning I was coming. I'm sure this is a shock."

Her smile turned a little watery, but she stepped aside to make room for him to pass.

Frowning at the fancy rug just inside the doorway, Wolf stomped off the week-old Iraqi desert still clinging to his boots and moved forward. The smell of furniture polish and old money had him hesitating. But only for a moment.

Shoulders back, he followed Hailey down a portrait-filled hallway. He tried to look anywhere but at Clay's sister. Easier said than done, especially considering the confines of the tiny corridor. Each step she took was dignified and regal, the perfect blend of confidence and class that came from a life spent in country clubs and expensive schools.

Wolf shouldn't be watching her so closely. It reeked of betrayal to his friend.

Forcing back a spurt of guilt, he focused his gaze on the wall of pictures. They were hung in a haphazard pattern that made an odd sort of sense. Some of the photographs were in large frames, some small. Some were yellowed with age, others much newer. But all had the common theme of family, stability and normalcy, things Wolf had never experienced in his thirty years of life.

His guard instantly went up.

Good thing, too, because in the next moment Hailey led him into a large room with fancy tables, ornate chairs and more photographs. Lots and lots of photographs.

He could handle the obvious wealth reflected in the expensive furnishings. But *this,* this shadowy sense of homecoming, left Wolf wanting things he couldn't form into coherent thoughts.

There was something about this room that put him on edge. The comfort that radiated out of every corner was a visible reminder of everything Wolf had missed out on as a child.

Great. Nothing like being the big stinkin' fish out of water in an already tense situation.

Hailey set her purse and coat on a chair, then turned back to face him. "Please, have a seat, uh... Lieutenant?"

"Captain," he corrected automatically, looking for a suitable place to sit. "It's Captain now."

Unable to settle, Wolf avoided the fragile-looking furniture and strode through the room with clipped, restless strides.

Now that he was here, facing Clay's sister at last, he didn't know how to begin.

At the beginning? The end? Somewhere in between?

Hands clasped in front of her, Hailey eyed the soldier pacing through the original parlor of O'Brien House, all the while trying to keep hold of her composure. Unfortunately, Captain Wolfson's nervousness was wearing off on her. Clearly he had something important to say, but he wasn't having much success in getting the words past his lips.

So she waited.

And watched.

He couldn't stand still for more than a few seconds at a time. His fingers tapped out a chaotic rhythm on his thigh. Her toes caught the uneasy cadence, until she realized what she was doing and stopped. Clay had been jumpy like this the first time he'd returned home from Iraq.

Clay. *Oh, Clay.*

Her heart lurched at the mere thought of her brother. Tears stung the backs of her eyes. How she missed him. She'd been so proud of his role in the Army, awed by his dedication, and inspired by his descriptions of the strides the military was making in Iraq. But then God had taken him home. And Hailey had been forced to examine her own life. She hadn't liked what she'd discovered about herself.

But that was in the past. She was a different woman now, with more conviction. Where Clay had set out to bring peace to the Middle East, she would do what was necessary to bring hope.

Lord, help me to honor my brother's sacrifice with my mission work. Let him not have died in vain.

Feeling stronger, resolved, she focused once more on Captain Wolfson. He looked at home in his Army camouflage and tan combat boots. What Clay used to call his BDUs.

As she waited for the captain to speak, Hailey silently congratulated herself on maintaining her composure.

When she'd opened the door to him earlier she'd almost lost it.

During that terrible, heart-stopping declaration that he'd been with Clay when he'd died the tears had pressed against her lids. Only one had escaped. She'd held the rest back. That's what mattered. As her mother had always said, an O'Brien woman kept her poise under *all* circumstances.

Oh, but it hurt to look at this man pacing through her home like a caged panther. With his dark hair, ice-blue eyes and direct gaze, Captain Wolfson was far too much like her brother.

Except…he was nothing like Clay. Hard. Yes, that was the word that came to mind as she gazed up at him. No. Not hard. Sorrowful. Wounded. A man with regrets.

She could stand the suspense no longer. "You said you have something important to tell me?"

He jerked at her voice and then his hand shot out, as though he was reaching for something. His weapon? Clay had reacted the same way whenever a loud noise surprised him.

"I'm sorry, Captain." She spoke softer this time. "I didn't mean to startle you."

"It's okay." He closed his hand into a tight fist. "I'm just a little low on sleep."

Possibly. But she doubted that was the cause of his jumpiness. She rose slowly, careful not to make any sudden movements. "You have something to tell me about Clay?"

"Yes. But sit back down." He gestured to the chair she'd just abandoned. "Please."

"If you'll join me."

He looked at several pieces of furniture, narrowing his eyes as he went.

Understanding dawned. "Clay didn't like this room, either." She allowed herself a short laugh. "He said it was too girly."

Wolf smiled at that. It was a quick, almost indiscernible lift of his lips, but a smile all the same. Unfortunately, the gesture made him seem somehow...sadder.

Shoulders set, he lowered himself to the love seat facing her. She could practically hear his thoughts colliding into one another as he leaned forward and captured her gaze with his. "You should know that Clay died honorably."

It was her turn to smile, grateful for those simple, straightforward words affirming what she already knew. "I'm glad to hear it."

"You're not surprised."

"Clay was an honorable man."

"*That* he was."

An uncomfortable silence fell over them.

Hailey swallowed. "Was that what you came to tell me?"

"No." He broke eye contact, but not before she saw the agony in his gaze.

This conversation was hard on him, that much was clear. Well, it was equally difficult for her. She still missed her brother. Desperately. He'd been the last of her living relatives. After six full months, she often found herself waking in the middle of the night with tears running down her cheeks.

But as bad as she felt over her loss, this man had watched Clay die.

Without thinking too hard about what she was doing, Hailey moved to a spot next to him on the love seat and took one of his hands in hers. When he didn't pull away, she squeezed gently. Her meeting at the church was no longer important. Giving this man comfort mattered more. Maybe, in the process, she would find a moment of peace, as well.

For several seconds, Captain Wolfson sat deathly still next to her, staring at their joined hands with his brows scrunched together. Confusion? Frustration? She couldn't read his emotions anymore.

And then a dreadful thought occurred to her. "Did something happen to Clay that the military hasn't told me? Something...classified?"

"No." He sucked in a harsh breath. "*No.* His death was senseless, but not unusual. Our Humvee hit a road-side bomb. Clay lived a few minutes longer than the other three soldiers with us."

The other three? Counting Clay and Captain Wolfson that made five men in the truck. "Are you saying you were the only one who made it out alive?"

"Yes." The word came out softer than a whisper. And so sorrowful.

Hailey clasped his hand a little harder. "I'm sorry."

He squeezed back, then lifted his gaze to meet hers. She gasped at what she saw in his eyes. Pain. Grief. And something else. Guilt, maybe? Was he suffering from survivor's guilt? She'd heard about the terrible emotion, but had never truly understood it.

Until now.

Lord, how do I help this man?

She wasn't trained for something like this. It was more than she could handle.

Just as despair nearly overtook her, Wolf's face cleared of all expression and he tugged his hand free. "Clay made one final request before he died."

A sense of dread whipped through her. She didn't want to hear the rest. Captain Wolfson had the unrelenting look of a man filled with resolve, the kind of determination a person got when he had to do *or say* something awful.

As afraid as she was to hear the rest, she had to ask, had to know. "What was my brother's last request?"

"He asked me to stop you from going to the Middle East."

Hailey shifted uncomfortably in her seat. "But…that doesn't make any sense."

In fact, the very idea was absurd.

Captain Wolfson rolled his shoulders, his gaze never fully releasing hers. "He was adamant."

"You must have misunderstood. My becoming a missionary was Clay's idea."

"Not in the end." He spoke the words in a hard, ruthless tone while his eyes—those sad, grief-stricken eyes—flared with raw emotion.

Hailey wished she didn't see the misery in him, didn't understand it and want to soothe it away. So she focused on what she knew for certain. "You're mistaken. Clay's e-mails said otherwise. I saved them all, including the one where he first encouraged me to start the application process."

"Yeah, well, he changed his mind." Wolf's tone hardened even more than before. "When he was bleeding out on the desert floor."

Hailey recoiled. "How can you say something so awful, so…*graphic?*"

"Because you're not listening to me." He rose abruptly, towering over her with his massive size. He looked every bit the warrior now, a man who had seen and done awful things.

Odd, but she wasn't afraid of him. Only confused. His words and attitude didn't match any of what Clay had said to her. "It's… I mean, I…"

"Hailey. Listen to me." His voice shook as he dropped to one knee. The gesture brought his gaze at eye level with hers. "Clay was right to send me. You can't travel to the Middle East right now."

"But—"

"*Listen* to me. It's not safe. Your brother didn't want you in danger."

She heard the plea in his voice, saw the conviction in his bunched shoulders. "But, Captain Wolfson, mission work is dangerous. Clay knew that. *I* know it, too."

"I don't care how prepared you think you are, you can't go in there alone."

She touched his shoulder, surprised at the tension she felt under her hand. "I won't be alone. I'll have others with me. And, of course, I'll have God."

"*God?*" His shocked gaze locked with hers. "The Lord can't protect you from IEDs."

She sighed at his vehemence, not to mention his very real anger at God. She had to make him understand the Truth. "If it's His will, He can. Besides, you're missing the point."

"No. You are."

Looking into Wolf's angry expression, Hailey knew words wouldn't get through to him now. But maybe a firsthand account would.

"Come to church with me this afternoon," she said.

He looked at her as if she'd gone insane.

"We're having a reception for some visiting missionaries," she explained quickly. "Including a couple who are permanently based in the Middle East."

He opened his mouth, probably to protest, but she

raised her hand to stop him from interrupting her. "No. Wait. Don't say anything yet. I want to make a deal with you first."

His eyes narrowed. "What sort of deal?"

"If you promise to listen to the Mulligans' story without judgment, then I'll promise to listen to your arguments with the same mind-set."

He looked at her for an endless moment. As each second passed, frustration filled his gaze. But then he shook his head at her and said, "You're not going to listen to another word I say unless I agree to this, are you?"

"Nope."

"You are one hardheaded woman, Hailey O'Brien." His tone held a hint of admiration.

"So I've been told, Captain Wolfson."

A moment of solidarity passed between them. And something else. Something pleasant, but not altogether comfortable. "So you'll come with me today?"

"Do I have a choice?"

"Not if you want me to listen to the rest of your arguments."

He smiled at her then, with the kind of stomach-twisting grin that turned his blue, blue eyes to a deep midnight. He no longer reminded her of Clay. In fact, the man was far too handsome for his own good. Hailey had to remind herself why he was here. He wanted to stop her from going to the Middle East.

"All right. You win this round, Hailey. For the next, let's say, two hours." He glanced at his watch. "I'm all yours."

I'm all yours. Hailey's heart kicked hard against her ribs. *I'm. All. Yours.*

Three simple words, spoken in such a matter-of-fact tone. But Hailey knew the battle was far from over.

Captain Wolfson had made a promise to her dying brother. He didn't seem like a man who would relent easily.

Of course, what he didn't know was that she'd made her own promise. To the Lord.

Chapter Two

Hailey stepped onto the front porch ahead of Captain Wolfson. Although she could feel his intense gaze on her, she managed to click the lock in place on the first try.

Gathering her composure, she turned to face him directly.

Their gazes locked, held. And held some more.

Her pulse did a little cha-cha before settling into a heavy, thick *thump…thump…thump.*

Something deep inside her, the part she'd ignored since Clay's death, recognized this man as a kindred spirit. Was it solidarity from a mutual loss? Or something more disturbing?

Either way, it wasn't supposed to be like this. She wasn't supposed to be emotionally involved with a man after only a half-hour acquaintance.

Yet, here she stood, blinking at him without a word coming to mind. As the silence lengthened, the cold, wet air encircled them, creating an illusion that they were the only two people left in the world.

She wasn't attracted to the man. Was she? No. He wasn't her type. She preferred artistic intellectuals who wore wire-framed glasses. Not big, strong, elemental warriors.

"Where are you parked?" she asked, pleased at her even tone. If her mother was still alive she'd be proud of Hailey. After all, O'Brien women always kept control of a situation, no matter how unusual, unexpected or emotionally charged.

"I'm three blocks that way." He angled his head to her left.

She lifted her eyebrows, fully aware that the city's layout didn't afford adequate parking. "You actually found an open spot on the street?"

"Yeah. Total cakewalk." He gave her a wry grin. "If you consider three passes down eight different streets easy."

Hailey heard a trace of humor underneath the frustration in his voice. He didn't seem angry about the inconvenience of finding a parking space, only mildly annoyed. That said a lot about his character.

Her brother's friend was a patient man, even when he was clearly exhausted.

She found herself intrigued by him all over again.

Hailey, no. Not your type. Remember why he sought you out today.

"Captain Wolfson—"

"Ty." One side of his mouth kicked up. "My name is Ty."

Oh, why, *why* did he have to turn appealing now, when she was working so hard to put him in the role of opponent?

A breathy sigh slipped out of her before she could stop it. "Ty, I—"

"Or...you can call me Wolf."

Wolf. Right. That's what Clay had called him. She

could see why, too. His eyes were just like a wolf's. Stark, emotionless, guarded. Maybe even a little scary.

"Who's afraid of the Big, Bad Wolf?"

He sighed, looking slightly disappointed in her. Clearly, he'd heard that one before.

Why had she said it, anyway? Maybe it was because his grin had made her feel like Little Red Riding Hood skipping unwittingly into the beast's trap.

She'd been wrong in her earlier assessment of the man. He wasn't elemental.

He was dangerous.

And when it came to men, Hailey O'Brien did not *do* dangerous. Ever.

It was important she remember that little factoid about herself. "All jokes aside, I think Wolf suits you best."

He lifted a shoulder. "Call me whatever you like."

"Well then, *Wolf,* do you want to ride with me?"

"No." He looked over his shoulder in the direction he'd indicated earlier. "I have my own wheels."

His answer was quick. A little too quick. "How can I be sure you'll show?"

"Because I said I would."

She recognized her mistake at once. Even without Clay's e-mails to attest to his character, the rough honesty and deep code of ethics Wolf lived by were obvious in his direct gaze and straightforward manner.

"I'm sorry." She broke eye contact, resisting an urge to dig her toe in the knothole at her foot. "I didn't mean to insult you."

"Apology accepted."

Before he could speak again, she rattled off the address for Faith Community Church.

He nodded. "I know the one."

Again, he surprised her. "You do?"

He didn't reply at first, merely stared at her. A battle seemed to wage behind his eyes before he said, "Hailey, this isn't my first trip to Savannah. I was at Fort Stewart six months before I was deployed to Iraq this last time."

"But Clay's e-mails said you two met in Iraq."

"We did. We became friends—" He stopped, shut his mouth, swallowed hard and then started again. "We became *friends* when I got transferred to his platoon twelve months ago."

She reached out to touch his arm but he shifted away and then started down the front steps ahead of her. Without turning around, he waited for her to join him.

Play it safe, use your head and never, never make a decision out of emotion. Those had been the rules the old Hailey had lived by before Clay died.

The *new* Hailey was a full-grown, twenty-six-year-old woman who lived by a different set of standards. She took risks. Lots of them. Well, not yet. But she would soon. When she boarded a plane to Iraq. Or Afghanistan. Or wherever the mission board sent her.

Deciding to start being brave right now, Hailey marched down the stairs, head held high, and faced Wolf. "I'll see you at the church in fifteen?"

"Just so we're clear," he began. "I'll meet your missionaries. I'll listen to their stories, but then you have to let me say what I came to tell you. All of it. Without interruption."

"That's the plan."

"Good. We understand one another." He turned to leave without speaking another word.

Oh, but she'd caught the grim expression on his face. And the unrelenting tilt of his chin. On the surface, the man looked like a hard, physical specimen ruled by his own prowess. But Captain Wolfson was no knuckle-dragger. He was intelligent, determined and loyal.

He was not going to come around to her way of thinking easily.

Sighing, Hailey watched him head down the sidewalk. Only then did she notice his slight limp. Had he been injured during the attack?

It was possible. After all, he'd been blown up by an IED. The muscles in her stomach twitched at the thought.

Lord, why have You brought this man into my life? Why now?

With effort, she folded her confusion deep inside her and headed toward her own car.

Twenty minutes later, Hailey steered into the parking lot of Faith Community Church of Savannah. A feeling of home washed over her.

Like most modern churches, FCC was a functional collection of brick, glass and steel. But despite its lack of worldly grandeur, Hailey always met the Lord here. Even during the dark days following Clay's death, she'd found comfort. And peace. Not from the building, but from her church family.

It was her turn to give back to others in need. A spurt of excitement twisted along her spine. She would no longer be on the sidelines, waiting her turn. Soon, she would be in the heart of the action.

Smiling, she exited her car at the same moment a motorcycle roared into the empty spot beside her. The snarl of the engine had her jumping back. Her hand flew to her throat and she flattened herself against her car.

Loud, obnoxious, danger-on-two-wheels—what sort of insane, *crazy* person rode a steel beast like that?

As soon as the question came to her, she noticed that the person climbing off the bike wore BDUs and tan army boots. Even before he removed his helmet, she knew whose face she'd see.

Didn't she already recognize the powerful set of Wolf's shoulders and the way he favored his left leg?

There was something so familiar about the man, something that made her feel both safe and uneasy at the same time.

Maybe it was because he reminded her of Clay.

Or…maybe not.

She took in a steadying breath and sighed. She might tell herself she liked the artistic type, she might even believe it in her head, but Captain Wolfson was a *man*. A warrior. A bona fide hero in BDUs.

It was hard not to be attracted to him.

Her twenty-six years of safe existence hadn't prepared her for someone like him, someone who made her question everything she'd ever known about herself and the very real need in the world around her.

Wasn't that the point of her decision to become a missionary? To live out her faith among people? After all, what good did a formal education and countless Bible studies do if she didn't put her knowledge to use in the real world?

And this man, the one pulling off a *motorcycle* helmet, was here to stop her from taking the next step in her Christian walk.

Fat chance.

Convicted all over again, she waited for Wolf to join her on the sidewalk that led to the front of the main church building.

They walked in silence.

Despite her best intentions, Hailey kept sending him

covert glances from below her lashes. She was aware of the man with a sharp-edged clarity that was downright disturbing. "You won't regret joining me this afternoon."

He made a noncommittal sound deep in his throat.

Ho-kay, so he was going to play it *that* way?

"I thought you promised an open mind?" she said, failing to keep her annoyance out of her voice.

"It's open." He tapped his left temple. "Wide open." He sounded sincere. But then he gave her a grin that could only be described as...wolfish.

Oh, boy.

Thankfully, she caught sight of a familiar face heading their way. Relief spread through her. "Look, there's J.T." She lifted her hand in greeting.

"Who's J.T.?" Wolf asked, his voice wary.

"Our mission's pastor."

"Right."

Hailey wasn't sure what she heard in Wolf's voice, but he didn't sound convinced.

His next words confirmed her suspicion. "He doesn't look like any pastor I've met before."

Hailey eyed J.T., trying to see him from a newcomer's point of view. "That's because he looks younger than he really is. Don't be fooled, he's in his thirties."

"It's not his age." Wolf narrowed his eyes. "It's something...else."

There was such gravity in his voice that Hailey felt the need to reassure him. "J.T.'s a good guy. You'll like him." She played her ace. "Clay did. They were friends. *Good* friends."

Before Wolf could respond J.T. pulled her into a tight hug. "Hellooooo, beautiful."

* * *

Wolf had thought he'd seen everything. He'd survived fifteen brutal years with a mean, alcoholic father. He'd lived on his own for the next fifteen after that. He'd faced insurgents, enemy fire and an IED. But he'd never confronted anything—or anyone—like Hailey's pastor.

Man of God or not, the guy was overly friendly with Clay's sister. In fact, *Pastor* J.T. hugged Hailey a little too long, with far too much enthusiasm.

Inappropriate. That's the word that came to mind as the two finally untangled from each other's arms.

When J.T. kept his hands on Hailey's shoulders, a white-hot ball of emotion roiled in Wolf's stomach. He ignored the sensation and detached himself emotionally from the situation. He was a master at compartmentalizing. It was a gift.

Besides, what did it matter whether he approved of the relationship between Hailey and her pastor?

It was none of his business, emphasis on *none*.

"J.T.," she said, "I have someone I'd like you to meet." Hailey shifted out of the pastor's reach—which was good—and turned those compelling green eyes onto Wolf. Not so good.

His breath tightened in his throat and that ball of emotion rolling around in his stomach tied into a tight knot.

So much for detachment.

"Wolf, this is J. T. Wagner, our mission's pastor."

Despite his instant dislike of the guy, Wolf shook J.T.'s hand. With his surfer-dude, spiky, sun-streaked hair, ratty cargo pants and rock-star T-shirt, J.T. looked like a grown man masquerading as a teenager.

Something wasn't right.

Other than a diamond stud in his left earlobe, the pastor wore no jewelry. Not even a wedding ring.

Yeah, Wolf had checked.

After another moment of inspection, Wolf realized why the picture didn't fit completely. Despite the civilian clothing, J.T. had military written all over him. It was in his stance and the way he moved.

A former soldier turned pastor. Talk about a walking, talking nightmare for a man who didn't want to discuss the military or what had happened in Iraq or anything to do with the good Lord.

Wolf had to give the guy points, though. J.T. didn't flinch under his scrutiny.

Hailey cleared her throat. "J.T., Wolf was a friend of Clay's. They were together in Iraq."

J.T. nodded at Wolf, and a moment of camaraderie passed between them. Wolf didn't know what to do with that. He'd decided to dislike the man, on principle if nothing else. But he realized that wasn't going to be as easy as he'd first thought.

"How long have you been home, soldier?"

"Since this morning."

J.T. cocked his head. "Did they have a welcome-home parade at Cottrell Field?"

Wolf rolled his shoulders uncomfortably. "I chose not to attend."

He'd told himself it was because he'd been focused on getting to Hailey and fulfilling his duty. But his reasons were more complicated than that.

Without Clay and the others marching by his side, Wolf didn't deserve a welcome-home celebration.

Had he seen that bump in the road, had he paid more attention to that sick feeling in the pit of his stomach that day, all four of his fallen friends would be here today.

He—

Hailey touched his sleeve, her soft voice breaking through his thoughts. "You didn't look for Clay's tree?"

"No." He hoped she'd leave it at that.

It wasn't that he hadn't tried to pay homage to his friend. But when he'd pulled alongside the long row of evergreens, one planted for each fallen soldier of the Third Infantry Division, Wolf had lost the stomach for it. Literally.

Disgusted with himself, for his self-indulgence as much as his weakness, he'd climbed back on his motorcycle and had headed straight to Savannah.

"You really are determined," Hailey said, shaking her head in resignation.

Wolf stared into her eyes, silently communicating his resolve. "I made a promise to a friend. I—"

A loud whoop of feminine shouts cut off the rest of his words. "Hailey, Hailey. There you are."

A group of teenage girls swarmed her, giggling and laughing at such a shrill decibel Wolf wanted to cover his ears with his hands.

"Come on, Hail. The program's about to start." One girl after the other tugged on her, buzzing around her like bees to a flower. "You promised to sit with us."

Hailey looked at Wolf with a question in her eyes.

"Go on. I'll find you later."

She hesitated, looking uneasy at the thought of leaving him behind. "Are you sure?"

"No worries, *Hail*." He winked at her. "I'll be right behind you."

She sighed. "If you're sure."

"Positive."

After a final glance over her shoulder, she turned

her full attention on the giggling girls. Three steps and her demeanor changed. She turned into one of them. She laughed and smiled and…was that a skip? Did the woman literally have a skip in her step?

A surge of unexpected anger had him gasping for a decent gulp of air.

Did she have any idea what her life would be like once she arrived in the Middle East? Did she not understand the dangers she was about to face, merely because she was an American *and* a woman?

She couldn't possibly be prepared for the culture shock. Most soldiers weren't, and they had training.

If nothing else, Wolf had to make her understand what she was getting herself into.

Not until Hailey disappeared inside a larger crowd did Wolf remember the man standing beside him.

He turned his head, only to discover that J.T. was watching Hailey, as well. The man's eyes were filled with an emotion that had nothing to do with friendship.

Were the two dating?

Was it any of Wolf's business?

Yeah, as a matter of fact, it *was*.

He'd promised Clay he'd keep Hailey safe. And safe meant safe. From *all* threats. That included the kind that came wrapped inside surfer-dude pastors.

Wolf nearly growled.

J.T. visibly pulled his gaze away from Hailey and refocused on him again. "So you were a friend of Clay's."

The words were spoken as a statement, an attempt perhaps to open up friendly conversation.

Wolf wasn't in the mood. "I was with him when he died."

"That's tough, man." Understanding flared in J.T.'s

gaze and something else, something tragic. "I…" He shook his head. "There aren't words."

Wolf recognized the haunted look in the other man's eyes. It was the same Molotov cocktail of nasty memories mixed with guilt he'd seen in his own mirror. "No. There aren't."

J.T. rocked back on his heels and then stuffed his hands into his pockets. He blinked once, twice. By the third try his expression cleared and the carefree pastor was back. "Welcome to FCC, soldier." He slapped Wolf on the back. "Now come with me. You can tell me about yourself while we head inside."

Yeah, as if that was going to happen.

Feeling trapped, he matched J.T. step for step. Something in the pastor's manner warned Wolf to brace for impact.

What had started out as a long day was about to get longer.

Chapter Three

All Wolf wanted to do was climb back on his bike and ride. It didn't matter where. As long as it was anywhere but here. He still had most of his forty-eight hours of leave left. He could go a lot of places in that amount of time, even within the hundred-and-fifty-mile limit they'd given all returning soldiers.

At least J.T. had quit with the probing questions and Hailey had stopped looking at him with all that distrust in her eyes. Like she feared he was going to bolt at any second.

Okay, yeah. He wanted to take off. But he'd made a promise to Clay's sister.

He wouldn't break his word.

Pulling in a tight breath, he settled back against the metal chair Hailey had saved for him. He managed to sit through the Mulligans' introduction before the fidgeting set in. He contained his twitching to a light drumming of his fingers on his thigh. But as the missionaries continued talking, nothing could stop the hard ball of dread clogging in Wolf's throat.

Open mind, Wolf. You promised Hailey an open mind.

He took another breath. Slow and easy.

"It's not numbers we're after," Harold Mulligan said. "It's hearts." The man paused, and then slid his gaze over the crowd with deliberate slowness.

Wolf took the opportunity to study the missionary. The man was just what he'd expected. Tall, scarecrow thin, middle-aged with sandy-blond hair and fervent eyes.

"No obstacles are too big for God," Harold continued, pulling his wife closer to his side with an affectionate little tug. "Patty and I go where the Lord leads us."

Patty smiled up at her husband. The woman could be anybody's mother, thanks to her plump figure, curly helmet hair and polyester pants.

Harold cleared his throat. "Patty and I are on a faith journey that will impact eternity."

Wolf blinked at that last sentence, only now realizing what was making him so antsy. Mr. Mulligan wasn't saying anything of substance. He was speaking in fancy rhetoric—one lofty, Christian cliché after another.

Yet, throughout the room, heads bobbed in agreement to each hollow statement.

Had Wolf missed something here?

"We're doing important Kingdom work," Patty added with just enough gravity to earn her…wait for it…another round of head bobbing from the crowd.

Wolf shifted, gritted his teeth. Swallowed hard.

Open mind, dude. Get your mind open.

"Our goal is simple," she said. "We want to expand God's Kingdom to unreached places."

Yet. Another. Platitude.

Wolf couldn't take much more.

Thankfully, Mrs. Mulligan turned her attention to

the open laptop on the table in front of her. "It's best if you see the people we've met for yourself."

One keystroke later and a PowerPoint presentation popped up on the screen behind her. In the perfect splash of added drama, a contemporary praise song blared through the computer's speakers.

For five solid minutes, photographs of men with haunted eyes and missing teeth, women holding impossibly small babies and children with lost appendages slid by on the big screen.

Unable to look away, unable to bear the sight of those sorrowful kids, Wolf's stomach clenched. It was one thing for the men and women of the U.S. military to put themselves in harm's way. That was their job, what they'd signed up to do in the recruitment office.

But the Iraqi children couldn't choose for themselves. They had no control. And IEDs didn't discriminate.

Wolf shifted in his seat.

Why did the missionaries have to show all those blown-up kids, he wondered?

Oh, yeah, right. He knew why.

This was propaganda. At its finest.

Even still, it was impossible to remain unmoved. Wolf swallowed a lump in his throat the size of a cannonball and proceeded to drum his fingers on his thigh. Faster. Harder. His foot joined the erratic routine.

Those kids. There's too many to protect. It's an impossible task.

The music hit a crescendo and Wolf glanced over at Hailey.

She was wiping at her eyes and sniffling. Her conviction was palpable, her passion for the wounded kids evident in the slump of her shoulders when one of their pictures hit the screen.

His job just got harder.

As though sensing his eyes on her, she glanced over at him. Helpless despair was etched on her face.

Wolf knew the feeling.

She gave him a wobbly smile. He smiled back, but he was pretty sure the gesture made him look less than enthusiastic.

Sighing, she reached out and covered his hand with hers, squeezed gently then let go. The light contact, though short, had a soothing effect on him—enough to make him relax against the back of his chair and focus once more on the missionaries' testimony.

All right, he admitted it. The Mulligans might speak in Christian clichés, but their hearts seemed to be in the right place. Wolf still wasn't comfortable with their presentation. It wasn't what they were saying that bothered him so much. It was what they *weren't* saying.

Not once did they mention the dangers that came with their posting in an "undisclosed location" of the Middle East. And didn't that say it all?

They didn't speak of insurgents or the bounties on Christian ministers' heads. They didn't allude to IEDs, except in the subtext—obviously the blown-up children got that way somehow. Bottom line, the Mulligans were giving only one side of the story.

Confused, Wolf searched out J.T. He spotted the pastor lounging against the door frame in the back of the room. His gaze was glued to the screen, his attention completely engaged.

What was wrong with the guy? Surely he saw the flaws in the Mulligans' presentation.

The missionaries made it sound as if living in the Middle East was some sort of fun-filled adventure, with the added benefit of helping people along the way. Oh, sure, the wife spoke of her loneliness and missing her church friends, but she said nothing—not one word—about burkas or the deep-rooted hatred for Americans.

And nobody in the room but Wolf seemed to notice the glaring omissions.

Lambs to the slaughter.

He couldn't take it any longer. "I have to get out of here."

Hailey's eyes widened. "But you promised," she murmured. "You said you would stay and listen to the whole presentation."

"I'll be back. I just need a moment. I need..." *Air.*

"I—" She cut herself off and then gave him a short nod. "Okay."

The woman was certainly playing nice. Wolf appreciated that, until she gave him "the look." The one people sent him in airports and other public places. That insulting mix of hero worship, horror and sympathy.

Wolf hadn't expected that from Hailey.

Oddly disappointed, he rose and stalked toward the back of the room. He had a bead on that bright red exit sign and nothing was going to stop him from leaving.

He stepped out of the room without incident. Unfortunately, he was able to enjoy only three minutes of freedom before J.T. had the bad manners to join him.

Well, all right. *Good.* Wolf had a few things he wanted to say to the pastor.

"What's up, Wolf?"

Straight to the point. This was Wolf's kind of conversation. "Those people in there. They aren't telling the whole story."

"What are they missing?" J.T. sounded clearly confused.

"Don't tell me you really send people onto the mission field that unprepared." Talk about blind faith. Even Joshua had dispatched spies into the Holy Land before engaging in battle.

"What do you mean by unprepared, *exactly?*"

All right. Maybe Wolf was wrong. Maybe he'd jumped to conclusions. Maybe the real presentation happened later. "What sort of training do you give your missionaries before they leave the country?"

"Training? Oh, you mean preparation." J.T. nodded in understanding. "Not to worry, Wolf. We don't send anyone into a foreign country without putting them through an extensive application process."

Application process? Sounded sketchy to him. "What does that involve, *exactly?*"

Clearly unhappy with Wolf's sarcasm, J.T.'s lips flattened. "The usual stuff."

Right. "Let's pretend I don't know what that is."

J.T. spoke slowly, patiently, as if he were talking to an imbecile. Which they both knew Wolf was not. "We make sure they have a heart for God and a love of His Word. That they understand their job is to plant seeds through relationships. You know, that sort of *stuff.*"

Now Wolf was insulted. "What about general knowledge of the region, the terrain, the culture? What about basic survival skills?"

J.T. looked at him oddly. "We have classes. They learn how to speak to the unchurched and how to build relationships through common ground." He was so cool, so in control.

So full of it.

"What about when things go wrong? Are they prepared for that?" Wolf frowned. "I know all about the random kidnappings and ransoms and…worse."

"There are always safety issues," J.T. admitted. "But we aren't naive *or* stupid. We don't send our people into the field alone. There's always a seasoned missionary from that region who guides them along the way, a person who knows the terrain and the culture and, yes." He held up a hand to stave off Wolf's argument. "That includes teaching them which areas are safe and which ones to avoid."

"What do you mean by 'seasoned'? As in a former soldier, or a cop or even someone who knows how to defend himself properly, someone who hasn't spent his entire life in country clubs?"

"Ah, I get it now." J.T. nodded sagely. "You're worried about Hailey going to the Middle East."

"Ya think?" Wolf wiped a hand across his mouth, determined to keep his temper in check. "The question is, why aren't you more concerned? I know you're former military, so don't bother denying it."

"Hadn't planned on it."

"Were you ever in Iraq?"

"I was there." J.T.'s voice came out flat, unemotional. *Hard.* "Three times. Afghanistan, six."

Nine deployments to the Middle East? Not possible. For regular Army, anyway. Which meant only one thing. J.T. had been Special Forces.

Now the guy's behavior really confused Wolf. "If you've been over there that many times, you gotta know how dangerous it is to send someone like Hailey into the region unprepared."

J.T. remained silent. Wolf could almost see the thoughts running through his head. The sorting, sifting, measuring.

Wolf waited, mainly because he could tell that whatever conclusion J.T. was coming to, the guy wasn't happy about it.

About time.

"Okay, Wolf, maybe you're right. What Hailey and the others on her team are gearing up to do is beyond our usual scope here at Faith Community Church." The admission came hard, if his tight lips and stiff tone were anything to go by.

Wolf let out a relieved breath of air. "So you'll help me discourage Hailey from going to the Middle East."

"No."

And they were right back where they'd started.

"But you just said I was right."

"I said *maybe* you're right."

Semantics? The guy was arguing over word choice?

"There are some things we have to leave up to God," J.T. added, his tone full of conviction. "We have to trust that His plans are bigger than ours and that His timing is always perfect."

"Now *you're* talking in platitudes?" Wolf expected better from a former Green Beret. At least a little more realism.

"Not platitudes. Truth. We haven't lost a missionary yet. Not on my watch."

Before Wolf could challenge him on *that* shortsighted rationalization, J.T. went back to thinking. He scratched his chin, but this time not a single emotion crossed his face.

At last he dropped his hand to his side. "I admit you make a good point. Sending missionaries into long-term assignments might require more than the usual preparation."

"Might?"

J.T.'s eyes narrowed in thoughtful consideration. "We could start with a series of classes on basic survival techniques and see where that leads us."

Okay. They were getting closer to the same page.

"That's not a bad idea," Wolf admitted reluctantly. *Very* reluctantly. After all, what J.T. suggested didn't solve Wolf's immediate problem—keeping Hailey out of the Middle East.

"And I think you'd be the perfect person to teach the class."

"Me?" Wolf's heart stopped a beat, and in that single instant he experienced all the pain, guilt and regret of the past six months.

He could not, would not—no, no, no—teach any class inside a church. It was hard enough to be here today. He could *not* walk into this building on a regular basis.

He wasn't that much of a hypocrite.

"You're the pastor, J.T. Shouldn't you teach the class?"

J.T. dismissed the suggestion with a flick of his wrist. "An active-duty soldier would be better." His lips curved at a shrewd angle. "And it might be just what you need, too."

"What's that supposed to mean?" Although, Wolf wasn't sure he wanted to know.

"It would be a chance for you to give back. And who knows, serving others might help you with your guilt."

Wolf's shoulders stiffened. "Who said anything about guilt?"

J.T. simply blinked at him, his gaze saying, *It's right there, soldier. In your eyes.*

Wolf looked away from all that wisdom and understanding. He didn't want an ally. Or a friend. His friends were dead.

And Wolf's guilt was something he had to bear alone, every day, over and over. No amount of churchgoing or talking or serving others would erase his failure on that Iraqi roadside.

But maybe—just maybe—teaching a survival class to a room full of out-of-touch idealists could serve the one goal Wolf might actually be able to achieve.

If he did his job correctly, with just the right spin, he could prove to Hailey how unprepared she was for a trip to the Sandpit.

"All right, J.T. I'll teach your class on basic survival skills, but only if Hailey signs up."

"She will. I guarantee it." J.T.'s grin turned smug. "All I have to do is use my influence on her."

Yeah, that's what Wolf was afraid of.

Hailey glanced over her shoulder, craning her neck in the direction of the door Wolf had disappeared through. He'd been gone a long time. J.T., too.

What were they doing? What were they discussing? Her?

And wasn't that the most self-centered thought she'd had all day?

Shaking her head, she concentrated once more on the pictures in front of her. The image of a young boy caught her attention. According to Patty Mulligan, he'd been blown up by an IED. And had lost both his legs.

Hailey squeezed her eyes shut, trying not to see her own brother similarly wounded. Or worse, broken and dying on a lonely desert road.

Oh, Clay.

She didn't hear Wolf return until he slipped into the seat next to her and whispered, "What did I miss?"

Her eyes flew open, but she couldn't allow herself to look at the man who had been with her dying brother. What must he have seen? How bad had it been?

Did she really want to know?

"You missed more pictures, a few stories," she mumbled, not quite looking at him, but not quite ignoring him, either.

"Ah."

She started to shift her gaze back to the screen, but something in Wolf's tone had her turning her full attention back to him.

Her heart skipped a beat. And then another.

Wolf looked...he looked...happy? No, not happy. Pleased. Captain Wolfson was pleased with himself.

Uh-oh.

He smiled, then. A big, carefree grin that made him appear more than a little dangerous. She quickly looked away from all that charm, highly disappointed at the effort it took her to do so.

At last the Mulligans' presentation came to an end.

Again, Wolf leaned over and spoke in her ear. "Well, that was certainly interesting."

Again she didn't like his tone. Nor was she overly fond of the way her body instinctively leaned toward his.

She snapped her shoulders back and sat up straighter. "What's that supposed to mean?"

"What?" One of his eyebrows traveled slowly toward his hairline. "I can't remark on the speech?"

Funny how his answer put her further on edge. "You know you didn't mean that as a compliment."

He shrugged, neither denying nor confirming her accusation.

Enigma. That's what the man was turning out to be. Brooding one minute. Tortured over some distant memory another. Smiling the next. He was full of secret pain and silent regrets. Oh, and charm. Can't forget the charm.

Hailey didn't like the way her heart yearned to peel away the hard layers to get to the real man, the one she glimpsed when he smiled, the person who needed her compassion and understanding.

What was wrong with her? Shouldn't her mind be solely on her upcoming mission work for the Lord? Especially here. Now.

J.T. rescued her by choosing that moment to address the room.

Hailey leaned forward, determined to pay avid attention to whatever her friend had to say.

Wolf started to speak again. She shushed him.

"Did you just shush me?"

"Yes," she hissed.

He chuckled softly.

J.T. thanked the Mulligans for their presentation, and then added, "Our guests will be available for the next hour to answer any of your informal questions. But before we break away, I want to let you know about a class I'm thinking about offering."

J.T. made eye contact with Wolf.

Wolf nodded in response.

"What was that about?" Hailey asked.

Wolf shushed her.

Well. Nervy. The man had some kind of nerve.

"It's been brought to my attention," J.T. continued, "that the church might want to offer a six-week training course in basic survival skills to anyone going on a mission trip."

An excited buzz rose in the room.

"Show of hands. Any interest in something like that?"

Dozens of arms shot into the air.

"Excellent. Look for an e-mail in the coming days," J.T. said before dismissing the group for a short break until the next missionaries took the stage.

Something felt off about what had just happened. Hailey blinked at Wolf. He smirked back.

"Wait a minute." She looked hard at Wolf, turned her gaze to J.T. then swiveled back to Wolf again. "Are you teaching the new classes?" Her heart clunked against her ribs at the thought.

"Maybe." He grinned. "Okay, yes."

"Because…"

"It's a good idea?"

She narrowed her eyes. "Why do I think your involvement in this is anything but simple and straight-forward?"

"Because you have a suspicious mind?"

"Not before I met you," she muttered.

Chuckling again, he rose and offered her his hand.

She paused, but then realized she was being rude. She accepted his assistance with her trademark graciousness.

When their palms pressed tightly together, a quick spark of…of…*something* skidded up her spine. Flustered, she pulled her hand free. "Let's, uh, let's go…go meet the Mulligans."

Had she just stuttered? Really?

"Sorry, Hail." He looked down at his watch, swayed as he did so. "Your two hours were up ten minutes ago.

I'm gone." He turned on his heel, making a beeline for the exit.

She followed him into the hallway. "You're walking away? Just like that? What about our agreement? Isn't it my turn to listen to you?"

"I'd love to stay." He tunneled an unsteady hand through his hair. "But it's been a long journey home. At the moment I don't have much talk left in me."

Of course. Wolf had only just arrived in Savannah. Today. "You must be exhausted."

"You have no idea."

She should insist he leave and get some sleep, right now, but she couldn't let him go with so much unsettled between them. "Let's have dinner together Friday night."

"Are you asking me out?" He looked surprised, but not altogether unhappy at the prospect.

"No." *Was she?* "Okay, yes. I want to talk about—" she lowered her eyes "—Clay." Which was true, just not the complete truth.

There was something else going on between her and this bold warrior, something that had nothing to do with her brother. Something that was distinctly theirs. But she didn't know how to voice any of that.

It was probably best not to try.

"Please, Wolf, I want to know more about my brother's life in Iraq." She sighed. "You're my only connection to him now. You…" Her words trailed off.

He touched her cheek softly. "All right, Hailey. Friday night works for me. I'll pick you up at seven."

She instantly remembered the motorcycle he'd roared in on. *"No."* She took a calming breath. "I mean. I, uh, I'll cook."

Which could end up being far worse. She was a notoriously bad cook. B-A-D. Bad.

Wolf didn't need to know that, though. She had three days to pick up a few basic culinary skills.

If she failed? Well, there was always takeout.

Chapter Four

Wolf was back in Iraq, on the road outside Baghdad. Clay had taken the driver's seat, as usual, even though Wolf had argued the point until he'd lost his voice.

The bump up ahead hadn't moved since the last time they'd taken this route. But it had grown larger, monstrous. The IED underneath the debris was impossible to miss. Yet Clay nosed the truck straight for the bomb.

"Look out!" Wolf shouted, his voice hollow in his ears.

Moving in slow motion, Clay turned to look at him. His features were distorted, his movements uneven. "Don't worry, Wolf-man, everything's under control."

But it wasn't.

The Humvee dipped, then lurched forward.

Wolf reached out to grip the dashboard. He came up empty.

His breathing quickened into hard, angry puffs. The acrid smell of death surrounded him. He swiped at his forehead.

Bang!

Bang, bang, bang.

Enemy fire. Coming at them fast.

Wolf ducked. The Humvee started its roll.

He grabbed for Clay, but he missed and hit the ground hard. The impact knocked the breath out of him.

He dragged in choking gulps of air.

Another round of gunfire exploded through the air.

Wolf reached for Clay again. This time he caught him. Clay shrugged him off. "Not me. Hailey." His face turned a dingy gray below the blood-smeared cheeks. "Promise me, Wolf-man, promise you'll save my sister."

"I will," Wolf vowed. "No matter what."

The rapid-fire shots came again. Faster. Louder. *Bang, bang, bang.*

Wolf looked frantically around him. His vision refused to focus. "Medic," he shouted. "We need a medic."

"Wolf."

The oddly familiar voice came at him from a distance, like an unwanted echo inside his head.

Bang. Bang.

"Wolf."

He peered into the darkness that had fallen over the desert. The landscape blurred in front of him.

"Wolf, come on, man." The voice came at him again. "I know you're in there. I heard you call out."

Wolf pushed to his hands and knees.

The ground turned slick under his sweating palms. Slowly the room came into focus. His mind cleared, inch by brutal inch.

Right. *Right.* He was home. Back in the States. In one of the apartments on post. And he'd had The Dream again.

Bang, bang, bang.

Wolf flinched, resisting the urge to take cover.

"Wolf!"

He rolled his shoulders forward, recognizing the low-pitched baritone at last. What was J. T. Wagner doing here?

Shaking off the lingering despair that always came with The Dream, Wolf shoved to a standing position. He moved too quickly and lost his balance. He grabbed for the desk, miscalculated, knocked over a glass, which proceeded to shatter into a thousand little pieces.

"You all right in there?" J.T. called.

"Yeah, yeah, hold on. Just hold on." Wolf ached everywhere, but forced his feet to move. "I'm coming."

He made two tight fists with his hands, breathed in slowly. Exhaled. Repeated the process until he was back in control.

Barefoot, he maneuvered carefully around the broken glass and headed toward the door.

With each step anger warred with confusion. What did Hailey's pastor want with him? And why hadn't the man used the modern convenience known as a cell phone? If J.T. could find out where Wolf lived, he could have gotten his phone number just as easily.

Wolf kicked aside the duffel bag he had yet to unpack and yanked open the door. "What?"

Unfazed by the rude greeting, J.T. skimmed his gaze over Wolf's rumpled form. "You look terrible."

No kidding. The weight of The Dream was still on his chest, like a living, breathing monster determined to drag him back to that day on the Iraqi roadside. Back to... Back to...

He pressed the tips of his fingers against the bridge of his nose. "What time is it?"

"1730."

Five-thirty? In the afternoon? "And the...uh, day?"

"Thursday."

Not good. So. Not. Good. He trooped to the lone window in the room and tossed back the curtains. The afternoon light assaulted him, the pain a physical reminder that he was alive. *Alive,* while Clay and the others were dead.

Wolf's eyes slowly adjusted, enough to see that the sun was making its descent toward the horizon.

Grimacing, he gripped the curtain tightly inside his fist, then let go. Darkness returned to the room, blinding him as effectively as the light had. "Guess I was more wiped than I thought."

Making an odd sound in his throat, J.T. flicked on the overhead light. "How long did you sleep?"

Wolf wiped the back of his hand across his eyes. "Twenty, maybe twenty-one hours."

"Ah."

Confused by this visit, Wolf turned to face J.T. The guy had moved a few steps deeper into the apartment. *Apartment* being a loose term for the seven-hundred-square-foot dump. The room was made up of cinder blocks, linoleum, a metal desk and a twin bed. But as dismal as the tiny space was, it was twice the size of the room he'd had in Iraq.

J.T.'s gaze drifted around the perimeter. "I take it you haven't had time to find a permanent place to live."

"Not yet." Wolf hoped J.T. was through with the questions. It was none of his business why Wolf had chosen to bunk in a barren apartment reserved for enlisted men and women.

"If you need help finding a place to live," J.T. offered, "I have a lot of contacts in the area."

"I'm good."

"Okay." J.T. leaned calmly against the wall next to

the door. A delusion. There was nothing casual about the guy.

"Why are you here?" Wolf asked.

J.T. didn't move away from the wall. He just kept... leaning. The guy did a lot of leaning. Strange that Wolf hadn't noticed that before.

"I thought we could talk about the survival classes you're going to teach at the church."

Yeah, right. Like that couldn't have been done over the phone. "Nothing more?"

J.T. didn't move, not an inch, but Wolf could see the man morphing into a pastor right before his eyes. Here it came...

"That's up to you."

Wolf sighed. Looked like FCC's young pastor had a new project. "I don't have anything I need to discuss."

"Whatever you say, but I've been where you are, Wolf, and I think—" J.T. stopped himself midsentence and started over. "Well, anyway, I spoke with the senior pastor about your class this morning. He gave me the go-ahead."

Wolf waited for the rest. J.T. hadn't made the twenty-mile trek to Fort Stewart to tell him something he could have relayed in a text message.

Pretending only a mild interest in his surroundings, J.T. inched his way around a camouflage backpack, the unpacked duffel bag and various piles of gear.

For the first time, Wolf noticed the slight catch in the guy's steps.

How had he missed that?

"If the classes go well we might consider turning them into an ongoing series."

"That's nice," Wolf said, his voice tight. J.T. was

clearly working his way around the conversation the same way he'd picked his way through the apartment.

"It would be a great ministry opportunity for a soldier."

And there it was. The guy's real agenda.

Wolf shook his head, his uncompromising glare relaying the message *No, no. Not me. Not* me. He already had a "ministry opportunity." And her name was Hailey O'Brien.

That was the one good thing about The Dream. Whenever it came, he always woke up more determined to carry out his promise.

"No pressure, Wolf," J.T. clarified as he perched on a corner of the metal desk. "For now, let's focus on your first class. I'd like to set it up for next Wednesday."

That soon? "Any specifics you want me to cover?"

"I'll let you decide."

Oh, J.T. was good, tossing the responsibility back at Wolf, making him engage in the task from the get-go. No pressure? Yeah, right.

An awkward silence fell between them. Wolf refused to be the first one to speak.

A mistake. J.T. steered the conversation in a personal direction. "What's your story, Wolf?"

No way were they going there. "I was wondering the same thing about you." Wolf shoved his hands into his pockets. "Why'd you leave the military?"

J.T. shrugged, oh so casually, but Wolf noted the closed-off look that filled his expression. Denial. Yep, he recognized that one immediately.

"I was called into ministry."

Wolf didn't buy it. "A soldier doesn't decide to leave the Army one day and become a minister the next," he challenged, suddenly very interested in what the good pastor had to say next.

"You're right. My decision didn't come overnight." He readjusted his position. The new placement of his leg looked almost unnatural. "Long story short, I'm a better pastor than I was a soldier."

Which raised a lot of unanswered questions. Like the fact that J.T. was sitting here. With Wolf. At Fort Stewart.

"How'd you get on post?"

The guy broke eye contact. "I drove."

"You know that's not what I meant."

J.T. sighed. "I was given a medical discharge two years ago." With slow, purposeful movements, he lifted the left leg of his cargo pants. The ratty hem traveled past a shiny, *metal* ankle and stopped midway up a plastic calf.

A prosthetic. Wolf drew in a sharp breath.

That kind of injury could easily turn a man bitter. Wolf had seen it happen often enough. But J.T. hadn't let his disability hold him back. Instead, he'd gone into ministry.

What kind of faith did that take?

More than Wolf would ever have.

An unexpected wave of awe and respect filled him. Despite losing a leg in combat, J.T. had a certainty that radiated from him. He knew his purpose in life.

Wolf didn't have convictions like that. Not anymore. Despite his recent promotion to captain, he didn't have any real direction, either.

He realized now, as he stared at the certainty in J.T.'s gaze, that he'd lost more than his friends that day on the Iraqi roadside. He'd lost his faith. And no matter how many Army chaplains quoted Romans 8:28 to him,

Wolf didn't believe God worked all things for the good to those who loved Him. Not anymore.

J.T. dropped his pant leg back into place and put on his pastor face. "My turn for a few questions."

Wolf nodded. J.T. was a brother in arms, one who'd had the courage to reveal his career-altering injury. Wolf owed him the same courtesy. "All right."

"Why did you seek out Hailey as soon as you arrived back in the States?"

Wolf forced down the litany of emotions the question awakened and focused only on words. Words he could do. "I made a promise to Clay, right before he died."

"You were in the Humvee with him, right?"

"Yeah." The heaviness in his gut, in his throat, in his very soul, threatened to choke him. The only way to control the unwanted sensation was to focus on the conversation. Except...

Clay should be the one talking to J.T. right now.

God had taken the wrong man that day.

Did the Lord make those kinds of mistakes? Was Wolf really supposed to be here? Or was he supposed to be—

"Go on. What did Clay ask you to do?"

Wolf swallowed. "He asked me to keep Hailey out of the Sandpit."

"But that doesn't make any sense," J.T. said. "Her becoming a missionary was Clay's idea."

"Hailey said the same thing." Word for word, in fact. Apparently she'd discussed her decision with J.T. In detail.

Which did *not* sit well with Wolf.

"Hailey let me read Clay's e-mails," J.T. continued. "They were inspiring and very convincing. I don't understand why he would change his mind so drastically."

Wolf knew why.

"Because of the way he died. In his last moments of life, he had an epiphany. He didn't want Hailey anywhere near IEDs."

"Even if what you say is true, what makes you think you'll change her mind?"

"Because I *have* to."

"You might not like what I'm about to say, but, Wolf, if the Lord wants Hailey in the Middle East, she'll end up there, no matter what you say or do to prevent her from going."

Wolf's stomach rolled at the thought. "I don't believe that." He blew out a hard breath. "I *can't*."

"I realize that." The disappointment in J.T. was tangible, but thankfully he didn't continue arguing his point of view. "So, you want to go over the details of your class now, or later, say early next week?"

Happy to focus on the new topic, Wolf searched for some shoes other than combat boots. "Now works for me." He found a pair of worn-out leather flip-flops sitting under the bed. "As long as we can talk over a burger."

At the moment, Wolf could use a little junk food. The Dream, not to mention the sparkling conversation he'd just suffered through with J.T., had left an empty feeling in the pit of his stomach.

"I'm starving," he added for good measure, just in case J.T. thought he was stalling.

"Me, too." J.T. opened the door and waved Wolf past. "After you, soldier."

Maybe J.T. would turn out to be a friend. A real friend. Then again—Wolf remembered how the man's eyes turned soft whenever the conversation turned to Hailey—maybe not.

* * *

At precisely 7:00 p.m., Hailey opened her front door and froze. She had to work to keep a sharp thrill from skidding up her spine. But, *wow,* Wolf cleaned up nicely.

He'd chosen to wear civilian clothes, which made him look approachable, and yet still very tough. The guy was one hundred percent alpha male. All power and grace and soldier-boy charm.

For a moment, she could do nothing but stare. He didn't seem to mind, so she took her time studying him.

His ensemble was simple. Jeans, a light blue polo shirt and a chocolate-brown leather jacket. His clean-shaven jaw and chiseled features made him look as if he'd just walked off a Hollywood movie set. But the pain-filled eyes made him look lonely. And maybe just a little bit lost. Wounded, even.

Yes, there was a reason why she'd searched Google for terms like *battle fatigue* and *survivor's guilt.*

Somewhere during her research she'd had a revelation. The Lord hadn't brought this man to her doorstep to help Hailey with her grief. But the other way around.

She was supposed to help *him.* But first she had to get her mouth working properly.

He broke the silence for her. "Hi."

"Hi, yourself." Oh, brilliant response. And wasn't she using all three of her degrees to their fullest?

Of course, he wasn't helping matters with his intense eyes and stiff shoulders.

Finding it hard to catch her breath, she lowered her gaze to the colorful array of wildflowers he held in his hand. "Are those for me?"

"They are."

What a sweet gesture. And an insight into his true nature. Wolf was a good guy, both considerate and thoughtful.

He gave her a lopsided grin. The man really was hazardous when he looked at her like that. And she couldn't stop staring at him. She was suddenly thinking of fairy-tale endings and Prince Charming on a white horse and...

What was wrong with her?

Hailey considered herself an academic, a thinker rather than a feeler. She was not the fanciful sort. She had a plan for her life, one that had no room for an active-duty soldier with a killer smile.

He thrust the flowers awkwardly toward her.

"Oh, uh, thanks."

She took the bouquet from him with a slight tremble. Their fingers touched. It was just a brush of knuckles, a mere whisper really, but her heart fluttered against her ribs.

"Please, come in." Holding on to a sigh—barely—she stepped aside for him to pass. "Dinner is almost ready."

The pleasant scent of sandalwood and spices followed him as he swept into the foyer. The heels of his combat boots skimmed across the hardwood floors. For a big man, he was exceptionally light on his feet.

But then he stopped abruptly and she nearly collided into him. "Oh."

She lost her balance.

"Careful." His hands gripped her shoulders gently, holding her until she was steady again.

"So." He lifted a single eyebrow. "Where, exactly, am I going?"

This time she did sigh. She'd forgotten he didn't know

the house. He seemed so at home. Maybe it was that confident stride of his, or that take-charge attitude. Or maybe it was just wishful thinking. "Follow me."

Resisting the urge to look over her shoulder, she led him into the kitchen. She'd set two places on the antique table in the bay window alcove.

He eyed the settings with obvious misgivings. "Fancy."

"It's the O'Brien family china and crystal. I always bring it out for special occasions." She smiled up at him. "I thought this qualified."

"That's, uh, nice."

She'd lost him. He'd put up that invisible barrier between them, the one that communicated things like "keep your distance" and "back off" and, her least favorite, "not interested."

She took a deep breath and let it out slowly. "Or we could eat out on the deck. Paper plates. Plastic cups. At this time of year we might have to contend with the cold, but there won't be any bugs."

"I don't mind cold."

"The porch it is."

Within moments, she had them settled at the table on the deck. The outdoor lights provided plenty of light. The sounds of traffic and laughing filled the air.

They ate in silence, which wasn't as bad as Hailey would have predicted. She liked looking at Wolf. Despite his fidgeting, a sense of peace filled her when she was in his presence.

As she'd warned, the temperature had dropped below fifty, which translated to bone-chilling cold to Hailey's way of thinking. Wolf didn't seem to notice, so she huddled inside her sweater and endured. He took his time eating, seeming to savor each bite.

Yet the tight angle of his shoulders told her he wasn't completely relaxed. Every few minutes he would run his gaze from left to right, right to left, instinctively checking for danger.

"How's the food?" she asked.

"Awesome." He shut his eyes and breathed deeply. "It's been a long time since anyone cooked for me."

Guilt, that's what made her set her own fork down. "I didn't make dinner."

He lifted his eyes to meet hers and she could see the barrier going up again. And just when they were making progress.

"You have your own chef." It wasn't a question, rather an accusation, as though he didn't have much use for pampered women.

She bristled. "Of course not. I don't have servants waiting on me hand and foot, if that's what you're implying."

His skepticism radiated in the air between them. "You clean this place all by yourself?"

From the disbelieving look on his face, she knew he wouldn't understand why she employed Mama Dee. Aside from the fact that Hailey allowed the historical society to use O'Brien House for special events and tours—and thus each room had to be spotless at all times—Mama Dee needed the money. She was a single mother with five kids under the age of fifteen.

"I know what you're thinking, Wolf, but I don't order out every evening. Tonight, well—" she lifted a shoulder "—I wanted to make sure you had something special to eat."

Shock, disbelief, wariness, they were all there in his gaze. "You wanted me to have something special to eat?"

"I did." She twisted her napkin in her hands. "My cooking skills aren't at a level where I could have pulled that off."

"I don't know what to say." Now he just looked shocked.

And she felt awkward.

Determined to lighten the mood, Hailey closed her hand over his. "You don't have to say anything."

"Yes, I do." He rotated his wrist until their palms met. He squeezed, held tight for a moment too long then released her hand. "Thank you for going to so much trouble. I'm grateful. But, Hailey, I'm a simple guy with simple tastes. I'd have eaten a PB and J with equal enthusiasm."

Happy the tension had lifted, she spoke without considering her words. "I'll keep that in mind next time."

"Next time." He smiled. "I like the sound of that."

"Me, too."

They stared at each other, neither speaking, neither moving. The way he looked at her with all that intensity and raw emotion in his gaze nearly did her in. "Tell me what your dream meal would entail."

He leaned back in his chair and, oh, yes, *finally,* his shoulders relaxed. "You promise you won't laugh?"

"Of course I won't."

"Pizza. The greasier the better. There aren't a lot of Italian restaurants in Iraq."

"No." She let out a short laugh. "I don't suppose—"

The squeal of tires sent Wolf jumping out of his chair. He spun around, looking frantically around him. Right to left. Left to right. He flexed his fingers then made a tight fist. His eyes had a wild look in them, yet he was very, very aware. Ultra-alert. Only after he took a few deep breaths, and then several more, did he start pacing the length of the deck.

Back and forth. Back and forth. When he started on a third pass, Hailey took charge. "Let's go inside. You can tell me about Clay over dessert."

Chapter Five

Shadows chased one another around in the kitchen, layering an eerie, desolate mood over what had started out as a promising evening. Despite the many deep breaths he took, Wolf's pulse refused to slow to a normal rate. Unease from the squealing tires still nagged at him. He drummed his fingers against his thigh and waited for Hailey to speak. To smile. To do...something.

She could at least turn on a light. But instead of reaching for the switch, she moved through the room, igniting candles along the way. The golden glow cast a romantic mood.

Had she done that on purpose?

Or was she trying to calm him with the soft lighting?

Either way, a strange, sweet feeling melted through him, permeating the steely place deep in his core no one had ever breached. Wolf had been alone so long he thought he'd gotten used to the solitude, maybe even craved it on some deep, unhealthy level.

But something in him had shifted. And now he wanted more out of life than merely existing from one day to the next. He sensed Hailey was the key to this change.

Which was too bad for him.

She was Clay's sister, aka off-limits.

It didn't matter that her presence soothed Wolf in a way nothing had since that day on the Iraqi roadside. It didn't matter that she'd known exactly what he needed when that car had startled him. What *mattered* was why he had come here tonight. Because of his promise to Clay.

He could almost hear his friend saying, *This is not a date, Wolf-man. Not. A. Date.*

Struggling to keep his mind on his real task, Wolf looked everywhere but at the beautiful woman in the kitchen with him. He was making a considerable dent in cataloging the items in the room—antique table, china, fancy stoneware, various pots and pans—when Hailey finished lighting the candles and turned to face him directly.

Their gazes locked and the air clogged in his throat.

He forced out a slow, careful breath.

Hailey O'Brien was a stunning woman, even in a simple pair of jeans and a sweater. Wolf knew he would find an expensive designer label somewhere near the waistband of those perfect-fitting jeans. And that pretty blue sweater had definitely cost more than he made in a month.

The woman had style, with the expensive taste to match, which only managed to punctuate all the reasons why she couldn't go to the Middle East as a missionary.

Feeling restless again, Wolf looked away from those mesmerizing green eyes locked with his. His gaze landed on a photograph secured to the refrigerator by two heart-shaped magnets. He squinted through the threads of golden candlelight. A man and woman stood arm in arm in front of a Christmas tree. Wolf stepped closer and realized he was staring at a relatively recent snapshot of Hailey and Clay.

They were both dressed in formal black, wearing their perfect smiles and classic good looks as comfortably as Wolf wore his BDUs.

"That's from two Christmases ago," Hailey said in a soft voice from behind him. "Right before his first deployment."

Wolf nodded, but remained silent. What could he say, anyway? *I'm sorry? Did you have a good time that night?*

"We used to throw a Christmas party every year," she continued. "It was a family tradition my parents started before either of us were born."

Family tradition. Those two words were everything Hailey stood for and Wolf did not. Consequently, his mind spun around one unrelenting realization.

The Lord had taken the wrong man that day.

Clay had had a reason to live, a purpose outside the Army. Wolf had neither. No family. No wife. Not even a girlfriend. And he certainly didn't have a sister determined to head into a dangerous war zone for her pie-in-the-sky ideals.

Which reminded him...

Hailey wanted to talk about her brother. Wolf wanted to talk about the Middle East. He'd do both with one conversation.

But not in this house. There were too many reminders of Clay surrounding them.

"It's still early." He faced Hailey straight on. He told

himself he needed to be able to see her expression, to read what was going on inside that beautiful head of hers, but the real reason was he couldn't look at Clay anymore. Not even in a photograph from two Christmases ago. "Let's go for a ride."

"A ride?" She took two deliberate steps away from him. "On…on your motorcycle?"

Her voice shook just enough to make Wolf forget about important conversations and painful memories and well, *everything*, except calming her concern. "No, Hailey," he said in a soothing tone. "I drove my car."

"You did?" Was that disappointment in her voice? Interesting.

"You want to ride on my bike?" Wolf couldn't have been more surprised.

Or more pleased.

The idea of Hailey sitting behind him, hanging on to his waist, trusting him to keep her safe around hairpin turns, brought forth all sorts of warm, fuzzy feelings. Disconcerting for a guy who didn't do warm or fuzzy. Ever.

Not. A. Date. Why couldn't he remember that?

"Well, actually…" A line of concentration dug a groove across her forehead. "I do."

She had a million doubts in her eyes, but she didn't back down.

Brave girl.

"You're sure about that?"

She gave him a careless lift of her shoulder. "A short spin around the block might be fun."

Oh, yeah, it'd be fun. He'd make sure of it. "How about next time? When we go for pizza?"

At the suggestion, everything about her seemed to relax. "That works for me."

Worked for him, too. And if he had his way, he would ignore his misgivings and make sure their "short spin around the block" *was* a date.

But tonight, he had a more pressing matter to address. One he wanted finished between them. Tonight. "Let's get out of here."

"Okay. I just need to get my coat and then we can go." She hurried out of the room.

"I'll take care of the candles and meet you on the front porch," he called after her.

"Sounds good," she tossed over her shoulder.

Wolf couldn't stop a grin from forming. The night was suddenly looking up. But then he remembered what lay ahead and his smile vanished. Flattening his lips into a grim line, he snuffed out the candles. With each puff of air he mentally clicked off the reasons Hailey couldn't go to the Middle East.

Insurgents.

Unstable governments.

IEDs.

Roadside bombs.

He no longer needed to remind himself this wasn't a date.

Curious as to where Wolf had parked his car, Hailey let him lead her down the front steps of O'Brien House. A cool breeze blew across her face. She could smell the damp in the air.

Night had completely blanketed the city with its inky stillness, but that didn't pose a problem in this part of town. Since Savannah was best seen on foot, street-lamps had been erected at close intervals along all the sidewalks in the historic district, giving tourists enough light to see the city's famous architecture.

There was so much illumination on Hailey's street she could practically count the leaves on the azalea bushes.

Unfortunately, the lighting didn't provide any relief from the cold. She shivered.

And then Wolf halted beside a car parked directly in front of her house and she shivered again.

Shock slithered slowly down her spine, skidding to a stop at the soles of her feet.

What had she gotten herself into?

Unable to speak, her eyes tracked over what had to be the saddest excuse for a muscle car she'd ever seen.

"This is yours?" she managed to croak past the tightness in her throat, trying not to let her dismay show.

Grinning like a proud papa, Wolf ran his hand lovingly over the roof. "Hailey, meet Stella."

It was years of training from her mother that kept her mouth from hanging open. "You named your car?"

"You bet I did." He gave the hunk of metal an affectionate pat. "This little beauty has been my only constant for the last ten years." He grinned broadly. "Isn't she great?"

"Sure…"

The car Wolf adoringly referred to as *Stella* looked ready for a permanent trip to the junkyard. Hailey squinted. Were those large, dark-colored patches splattered over the hood rust marks? Dirt? A combination of the two?

"Are you sure that thing…er, Stella…is safe?"

"Have a little faith." Wolf leaned in close enough for her to smell his spicy, masculine scent and tapped her lightly on the nose. "Stella might be in desperate need of a paint job, but the old girl is in her prime."

Hailey slid a skeptical glance over the car—hood to tail, tail to hood. "I'll have to take your word on that."

"Come on, sweetheart, where's your sense of adventure?"

"I think I left it in the house." She deliberately turned her back on the car. "Maybe I'll just head inside for a moment and look for it."

Chuckling, Wolf swung her back around with a gentle hand on her shoulder. "No way are you bailing on me now. You've come this far. Might as well go the distance." He opened the car door for her. "Go on. Climb in. Stella doesn't bite."

"I'm going to hold you to that." Heaving a dramatic sigh, she lowered herself into the passenger's seat.

The crisp smell of lemon and new-car scent surrounded her. A single glance at the car's interior and Hailey took back every negative thought she'd had about Stella.

Delighted, she rubbed her hand across the butter-soft, blue leather seats and then eyed the shiny, chrome-plated dials.

Wow!

Wolf had clearly spent considerable time and money on restoring Miss Stella's interior. Afraid to touch anything, Hailey perched on the edge of her seat, folded her hands in her lap and waited for Wolf to walk around to his side of the car.

Now that her initial Stella-shock was wearing off, something Wolf had said earlier came back to mind. The moment he settled in behind the steering wheel, she addressed the issue head-on. "You mentioned that Stella has been your only constant for the last ten years. Does that mean you don't have any family?"

"That's right." Staring straight ahead, he placed his hands on the wheel at the ten-and-two position.

The tone of his voice told her not to press the subject. She did anyway. "Not even a distant cousin?"

"No, Hailey." His hands clutched the wheel tighter. "No one. The Army's all I've got."

She recognized the emptiness in his voice, understood the bleakness it represented. The emotion was so similar to what she felt herself that her heart skipped a beat. Yet even as she empathized with Wolf, she sensed his loneliness wasn't as straightforward as hers. She feared his past held something dark, something she could never truly understand.

Should she quote Scripture to him at this point, or maybe recite words filled with God's truth about His unfailing love?

No. Something in the way Wolf held his body slightly away from her, almost isolated, didn't inspire her to introduce the fundamentals of God's love into the conversation.

Except...

What if she started by addressing the one thing they had in common? "I guess we're both alone in this world."

He made a noncommittal sound in his throat, one that clearly said the topic was closed. Without looking at her, he turned the key in the ignition and Stella roared to life.

Hailey gasped as a succession of grinding metal, snarls and rumbles whipped through the air.

Wolf pressed down on the accelerator. Stella responded with a loud, menacing growl.

Gasping again, Hailey braced her hands on the dashboard and hung on for dear life.

Stella wasn't through. She shook. She shimmied. Until, finally, "the old girl" descended into a vibrating rumble.

Needing a moment to collect herself, Hailey shut her eyes. She couldn't think past the blood rushing in her ears. Or was that terrible noise coming solely from the car?

"Ready for a sweet ride?" Wolf asked.

No! She slowly opened her eyes. *Be brave, Hailey, be brave.* "Sure."

He put Stella into gear and pressed on the gas pedal. Surprisingly, the car's engine settled into a low-pitched purr as she slid away from the curb.

After several blocks of pitch-perfect propulsion, Hailey grudgingly admitted that Miss Stella did indeed give one sweet ride.

Relaxing enough to unclench her fingers, Hailey settled back against the soft leather of the comfortable bucket seat. "Where are we going?"

"I thought we'd head out to Tybee Island."

He wanted to go to the beach? So soon after returning home? "I would think you'd be sick of sand by now."

Clay had avoided Tybee for months after his first deployment.

"I am." A grim look crossed his face. "But I haven't had nearly enough water."

Of course. "That makes sense."

"Besides." His expression lightened and he hooked his wrist over the top of the steering wheel. "It's a pretty drive."

"You think so?" She couldn't say she particularly agreed. "The road is nothing more than a causeway that cuts through the marshes."

"Exactly."

She narrowed her eyes, confusion gathering inside her. "I don't follow."

"There isn't a lot of marshland in the desert."

"No. I suppose not." She should have realized that on her own.

After several moments of Wolf concentrating on the streets and Hailey watching him out of the corner of her eye, they broke free of Savannah.

For the next five or so miles, Hailey tried to look at the familiar scenery from Wolf's perspective. Not an easy thing to do. The marshes were just plain spooky under the silver light of the full moon. Even with the windows rolled up against the cold, the tall grasses were ripe with the smells of mold, mud and rotting fish. It was a perfect hunting ground for gators and snakes.

Hailey shivered yet again, which was really quite enough of that.

She had to admit, though, words like *Middle East* and *desert* did not come to mind as the scenery whizzed past in a blur. As a matter of fact, Miss Stella seemed to be gobbling up the road a little faster than Hailey would have thought possible.

From under her lowered lashes, she checked the speedometer. Eighty-five. *Eighty-five?*

A rush of adrenaline surged through her blood. *Breathe, Hailey. Just breathe.*

"Are we late for something?"

"No. Why?"

She pointed to the speedometer, trying not to give in to panic, but—*oh, my*—he'd just pushed their speed past ninety.

"We're going a little fast, wouldn't you say?"

He flashed her that quicksilver grin of his, the one

that had her thinking of big, bad wolves. "I like fast," he declared.

Afraid to take her eyes off the road, Hailey white-knuckled her seat and stared straight ahead. Okay, yes, the causeway was a long stretch of uninterrupted highway. And there were no other cars out tonight.

But still…

Wolf must have sensed her agitation. "Are you all right?"

"Fine. Never better." She dug her fingers deeper into the soft leather of her seat, but she didn't take her eyes off the road. Blinking was simply not an option. "Having loads and loads of fun over here."

"Uh-huh."

"All right, Wolf, let's face it. There's fast and then there's fa-a-a-ast."

He chuckled, but immediately eased up on the gas pedal. "I know what I'm doing." He patted her hand. "Trust me, sweetheart."

Oh, sure. Trust him. That was just soooo easy to do when she was sitting in a muscle car with a guy named *Wolf,* traveling faster than she'd ever gone before.

The best she could do was *not* talk. And maybe watch the scenery. What little she could decipher.

She caught a flash of…something rush by on their left. She figured the quick burst of light had come from Fort Pulaski. The historic Civil War fort sat on a tiny island between the Atlantic Ocean and the Savannah River.

"You can relax your spine a little. We're nearly there," he announced.

"Praise the Lord!"

Only after he eased up on the accelerator again did she slant a glance in Wolf's direction. The bright moonlight revealed his features clearly, enough that she could see his brows scrunched in concentration. Obviously he was contemplating his next words very carefully.

"You might be interested to know I ate lunch with your pastor the other day," he said at last.

"You did?" She wondered when he'd had the time to meet Keith Goodwin, Faith Community Church's senior pastor, then remembered the e-mail she'd received this afternoon. "Oh, you mean J.T."

"We hammered out most of the details for the survival classes I'm going to teach at your church."

"That explains why he sent out a blanket announcement encouraging everyone taking a mission trip to attend. The class starts next Wednesday, right?"

"Yep." He proceeded to beat out a complicated beat on the steering wheel. "Will you be there?"

"Wouldn't miss it."

He fell silent for a moment. Thanks to the close confines of the car, she could feel the tension in him.

"Tell me why you want to be a missionary," he blurted out in a rush.

She sighed heavily. "That was certainly straight to the point."

"Maybe. But we've put off this conversation long enough. You know why I agreed to come to dinner tonight."

No, actually, she'd forgotten. She'd settled into the evening as though they were on a first date, explaining away the awkward moments to the usual getting-to-know-one-another jitters.

She wouldn't make that mistake again.

"Yes, I know why you're with me tonight." She ignored the sting of rejection building into tears behind her eyes and continued. "You think you have to convince me to stay out the Middle East."

"There's no 'think' about it." He slowed yet again, enough to swing Stella down an alley leading to beach access. He slid the car into a parking place under a low-burning streetlight and then cut the engine. "But I promised you an open mind and that's what you'll get from me."

He sounded sincere. She wasn't sure she believed him.

"Help me to understand your motivation, Hailey."

"Why?" She frowned at the shadows dancing across Stella's hood. "So you can use the information against me?"

"I wouldn't do something that low. I'm really interested in your answer. What can I say?" He gave her a crooked smile. "You intrigue me."

Glowing from the unexpected compliment, Hailey held back a gasp of pure feminine pleasure. Suddenly the interior of the car felt too small, too intimate. It was hard to think coherently with this handsome soldier sitting next to her. "Let's discuss this on the beach. I tend to think better when I'm walking."

He gave her what she was starting to consider the "Wolf" look and then reached for the door handle on his side of the car. "Whatever will make you most comfortable."

His tone sounded so rigid, the angle of his jaw looked so implacable, Hailey feared he thought she was trying to put off answering his question.

She picked at a speck of white fluff on her sleeve, wondering what he would think if he knew the real reason for her suggestion. She wasn't stalling. She was merely finding it hard to keep her mind on her goals with his masculine scent teasing her nostrils and his presence scrambling her thoughts.

But as far as her calling to become a missionary? Well, Wolf would either understand her reasons or he wouldn't. No matter what he said or did, he would *not* convince her to stay out of the Middle East.

Forcing down any last remnants of unease, Hailey summoned a brisk air of confidence and climbed out of the car.

Game on.

Chapter Six

Hailey started down the beach several feet ahead of Wolf. The full moon cast a brilliant, silver streak of light over the ocean, while the scent of salt water and sand clung to the cold air. Waves broke onto the shore in perfectly timed intervals, creating a sound track for their walk. But with so many thoughts working around in her brain, Hailey couldn't enjoy the scenery.

The sand squeaking under Wolf's feet alerted her to his progress. He caught up with her just as she paused to watch a transport ship ride the distant waves. Its large, guiding light bobbed up and down as the vessel tracked slowly toward the horizon.

Now that the time had come to tell her side of the story, her heart pumped wildly against her ribs. Or was her reaction because he was once again standing so close...*too close?*

She slid a quick glance in his direction. He carried himself with an unmistakable air of seriousness. His gait was stiff and careful, as though the soft sand presented a slight challenge for him.

Again, she wondered if he'd been wounded in the roadside bomb attack and whether or not he had a lingering injury. One that acted up in the damp beach air.

Of course, now probably wasn't the best time to ask him. She'd stalled long enough. "If I'm going to explain where I am and where I'm heading, it's important you know where I come from."

"I know where you come from." His voice matched his stiff gait. "Generations of family tradition, with the kind of long-reaching roots that didn't just start a few years ago but *centuries* ago."

He didn't sound impressed. On the contrary, his voice held a note of censure.

She stopped walking.

He did the same.

The moonlight gave her enough illumination to see his face clearly. The sharp angle of his jaw made him look harsh and unforgiving.

"You hold my upbringing against me." She all but gasped out the words.

"I'm trying not to."

A part of her appreciated his honesty, but the obvious doubt in his tone told her he wasn't having much success.

Hailey gave him a bewildered shake of her head. "Why is it wrong to come from an old family, to have solid roots?"

He twisted his stance to look out over the water, shutting her out as effectively as if he'd completely turned his back to her. "There's nothing *wrong* with it. It's just not something I have much experience with. My family wasn't exactly like yours."

Something in his tone alerted her to tread carefully. "No?"

He continued looking out over the water. "Let's just say my childhood wasn't as…secure as yours."

His softly uttered words said it all. Clearly, Wolf's parents—one or both of them—had let him down in some terrible way. Although she didn't know the specifics, her heart took a painful dip in her chest for all that he'd suffered. And, yes, she had no doubt he'd suffered.

"I'm sorry, Wolf." What more could she say?

"I believe you are." He turned and closed the distance between them—literally and figuratively. The barriers he'd erected earlier were gone. Completely. He'd simply let them drop and was now looking at her with stormy emotion waging a war in his gaze.

Hailey felt honored that he trusted her enough to let her see all that raw pain. And yet, she was petrified she would somehow let him down. He kept so much inside him she had no idea how to proceed. Or what words to use.

Fortunately, she didn't have to say or do anything, because in the next moment he took her hand and cupped it protectively in his. She watched, fascinated, as he stroked the pad of his thumb across her knuckles. Once. Twice. Her heart did another quick flip at the same moment he twined his fingers through hers.

"Tonight isn't about me or my dysfunctional childhood," he said at last, still staring at their joined hands.

Perhaps any other time Hailey would have agreed with him. But if she'd learned anything in her countless Bible studies, it was to go in the direction God nudged her. At the moment, she felt a strong shove toward Wolf. "Maybe if you told me—"

He spoke right over her. "Go on, Hailey, help me to

understand your desire to become a missionary. And don't use fancy clichés like we heard from the Mulligans. I want honesty from you."

He was so large, so intense, so...*close*. Yet fear wasn't the first emotion that ran through her. It was a strange mix of excitement and fascination. Like he'd claimed about her earlier, the man definitely intrigued her. "All right. If that's what you want."

"It is."

In silent agreement, they resumed walking, still holding hands. Even though her instincts warned her not to get too comfortable, the connection between them felt so natural, so familiar, Hailey didn't try to pull away.

"Just like you said, I come from an old Savannah family, with solid roots and a legacy that can be traced back to the seventeen hundreds. There's always been wealth and privilege in my family. But don't think that means the O'Briens have ever taken their blessings for granted. My mother in particular took her position in society very seriously. She spent her entire life dedicated to her causes. She—"

Hailey cut off her own words, a sense of loss and frustration mingling inside her. She knew she would never fill her mother's shoes. And, much to her shame, there were moments when she was glad for it. Sitting on charity boards and supplying funds for various causes had never been satisfying. Unfortunately, it had taken Clay's death to reveal that truth to her.

With a gentle tug on her hand, Wolf slowed their pace. Hailey hadn't realized she'd sped up.

"What about your father?" he asked. "Tell me about him."

Glad for the change in topic, Hailey smiled. "He was the senior partner in the law firm my great-grandfather founded. Daddy was a really good lawyer but he was an even better father. He was kind, loving, firm yet fair."

"You were fortunate, then."

"I was," she said, pausing to decipher what she heard in his tone. Bleakness? Envy? If only he would tell her more about his past. If only she could read his expression and decipher his secrets for herself. But the moon had slipped temporarily behind a cloud.

Wolf cleared his throat. "Clay mentioned your parents were killed in a plane crash."

Instant pain unfolded in her chest and threatened to crowd out the breath in her lungs. Hailey *couldn't* give in to her grief. Not in front of Wolf.

She inhaled a ragged swallow of air and said, "My father was flying the company jet. My mother was his only passenger. They were coming to a University of Georgia football game. Clay and I were waiting for them at a private airport in Athens. We were supposed to all sit together at the game. I… We…"

Before she realized what he was doing, Wolf swiveled in front of her and caught her up in his arms. "I'm sorry, Hailey. Losing both of them at the same time." He made a sympathetic sound deep in his throat. "That had to be tough, especially with parents like yours."

With Wolf's strong arms wrapped around her, Hailey gave up fighting the onslaught of emotions demanding release. Sighing, she rested her cheek on his shoulder and let the sorrow come.

After a few endless moments of gasping for air, she was able to continue. "As hard as it was to lose them, losing Clay was harder." A series of silent sobs wracked through her body. "He wasn't just my brother. He was my best friend."

Wolf's embrace tightened. "Clay was the best man I ever met."

She smiled into Wolf's muscular shoulder. The leather jacket felt cool on her cheek. "Of course he was."

Murmuring an unintelligible response, he dropped a kiss on the top of her head.

After several minutes of Hailey clinging and Wolf rubbing her back soothingly, he set her away from him. The cold, damp air slapped her in the face.

They set off down the beach again. This time, Wolf didn't take her hand. The lack of connection left her feeling isolated and alone.

"I know Clay joined the Army after your parents' plane crashed. What about you, Hailey? What did you do after they died?"

"I finished college with a degree in Latin and one in Greek. Then I earned another in Classical Literature." She kept her voice even, or as even as she could under the circumstances.

"I take it you like learning."

She shrugged. "With my parents dead and Clay in Iraq, school was my only lifeline, the only thing I knew."

"Understandable."

Why did he have to be so sweet? When he was here for all the wrong reasons? "Anyway, one of my professors told me I couldn't take classes forever, not without an end goal in mind."

"He kicked you out?"

Wolf's outrage made her smile. "Not exactly, but *she* didn't encourage me to stay, either. Since I didn't really know what I wanted to do with my life, I came home and took over my mother's charity work."

"Is that when you decided to become a missionary?"

"No." She abruptly changed direction and ambled toward the water's edge. This was where the conversation got hard.

She pulled in a sharp breath. "There was something still missing. At Clay's urging, I joined Faith Community Church and started taking Bible studies." She dug a toe in the wet sand, kicked a ball of white foam in the air. "Within a year I could rattle off Scripture as well as any trained pastor."

Wolf drew alongside her. "That's a bad thing?"

"It was for me. I'd intellectualized my faith. Clay kept pushing me to get my hands dirty, but I didn't know what he meant. And then…" She paused until she was certain she could speak without her voice breaking. "He died."

Just saying those two horrible, awful, *painful* words, tears welled in her eyes. She held them back with a ruthless blink and turned her head to look at Wolf. Even under the muted moonlight she saw her own sorrow mirrored in his gaze.

That gave her the courage to finish with the honesty he'd requested. "Not long after his death, I realized what Clay meant. I was just playing at being a Christian."

"Doesn't seem that way to me."

"Come on, Wolf. Don't you understand? Having a heart for causes is *not* the same thing as having a heart for people. The truth is…" She choked back a sob. "I'm a fraud."

Wolf stared into Hailey's eyes. They were bright with unshed tears. He'd never seen such self-recrimination, or such conviction to change. Except, possibly, when he looked in his own mirror.

Willingly or not, Hailey had just revealed her greatest fear—that her life was meaningless and without purpose.

Wolf had lived with that particular terror himself. He'd lost everything that day in Iraq. His brothers in arms, his best friend, even his purpose. Or rather his surety in his future with the Army.

He'd been questioning his life choices ever since. Rightfully so. But in Hailey's case, she was dead wrong. "You're no fraud. You're the real deal."

"Not yet." She swiped the back of her hand across her eyes and sniffed. "But I will be."

"Don't do this to yourself. I saw you in action the other day, with those teenage girls. You touched their lives right in front of me."

"It's not the same."

"Why? What's wrong with helping people in your own church?"

"It's not enough." She batted at a strand of hair that had fallen over her face. "Not *nearly* enough."

"Oh, I get it now." He laughed without a stitch of humor. "You think risking your life in a foreign land is the only thing that will make you a real Christian."

"I didn't say that."

"You didn't have to."

Her expression turned stormy. "You're intentionally misunderstanding me."

Not even close. "Look, Hailey, giving men and women a uniform and a gun doesn't make them soldiers. Nor will hopping on an airplane and flying to the Middle East make you a better Christian."

Her head snapped back as if he'd slapped her. "My brother thought otherwise."

A high-definition image of Clay's pale face insinuated itself into Wolf's mind. For one black moment, he was tempted to give Hailey all the gory details of her brother's death. The sights, the sounds, the terrible smell of blood that haunted Wolf in his dreams.

"No, Hailey." The effort to restrain himself had his words coming out hard and fast. "Clay didn't believe that for a second."

"He did. I have his e-mails to prove it. He died because he believed in the Army's mission. I have to honor that. I have to honor him."

The sheen of tears in her eyes gave Wolf pause. But only for a second. "How do you plan to do that? By dying for your beliefs, as well?"

"You're being intentionally obtuse." She wrapped her arms around her waist and stared out over the water. "J.T. understands my motives. Why can't you?"

Overwhelmed by an intense surge of jealousy at the mention of J.T.'s name, Wolf's jaw tightened of its own accord. He swallowed. *Hard.* Then forced his teeth to unclench. "Don't mistake a guy's romantic interest in you with understanding."

Her head whipped toward him. "It's not like that between J.T. and me."

"It's *always* like that."

She spun away from him. "I'm through with this conversation."

"Well, I'm not." He reined in his temper enough to walk calmly around her. "Despite what you think, Clay isn't looking down from heaven waiting for you to prove you're as courageous as he was. His last request was to make sure you stayed safe. I'm here to ensure that happens."

Her stubborn expression returned. The silence lengthened to an uncomfortable amount of time. In that moment, with her eyes telling him she would *not* back down, Wolf realized more arguing on his part would hurt his cause.

A smart soldier knew when to walk away, or at least when to build a different plan of attack. "How many mission trips have you gone on?"

Making a sound of dismay in her throat, she tried to maneuver around him.

He blocked her retreat. "How many?"

She lowered her gaze. "One."

"That's it?"

"It was enough," she said to his feet. "It made me hungry to do more."

Which was admirable, in its own way. Yet the question still remained. Why the leap from a short mission trip to a permanent posting in the Middle East?

"Where did you go on your *one* trip?"

"Jamaica." She slowly raised her head. "For two and a half weeks. And I'm heading to Haiti in a few weeks. I'll be there for seven days."

Wasn't that just *great*. The woman was basing a life-altering decision on practically zero field experience. The Army would never send a soldier overseas with such a gross lack of training.

"A Caribbean island is nothing like the Middle East."

"I know that."

"Do you?"

Moving quicker this time, she twisted around him and began retracing her steps back to the car.

Wolf followed hard on her heels. "Hailey—"

"Don't." She thrust her palm in the air between them. "I have the money, the time, the desire. It's not like I'm leaving anyone behind. Now that Clay is gone, I don't have...*anyone*."

The catch in her voice broke his heart. "You have your friends and your church." But even as the words slipped out of his mouth, Wolf knew how empty they sounded. Hadn't he hated hearing them all his life?

His frustration was making him careless. Why couldn't the stubborn woman see she was making a mistake?

"Hailey, I admire your passion." At her skeptical glare he added, "I do. But you won't be heading into a mission field that's been well traveled. There are bad men over there with guns, men who hate women like you."

"What do you mean women like me?"

"*Christian* women."

"That doesn't mean I shouldn't go." Her feet moved faster, kicking up large sprays of sand as she went. "Someone has to reach the desperate people living in that region. Why not me?"

He could give her a thousand reasons. He focused only on the main two. "Because you don't have the training or the experience."

"I'm getting both." She pumped her legs faster. "Step one was Jamaica. Step two is Haiti. Step three...well, God will reveal that to me in time."

Wolf easily kept up with her, even though his frustration made his steps jerky. "Hailey—"

"Stop worrying about me. When the door finally opens to the Middle East I'll be ready."

"You don't have an assignment yet?"

"No."

Well, that was new information. Maybe, just maybe, Wolf was going about this all wrong. From her own admission, Hailey wasn't scheduled to leave for the Middle East anytime soon. And she wasn't leaving for Haiti for several weeks. That gave him time to show her just how unprepared she was.

Ideas came fast now. But at the moment, he didn't bother sorting through them. He had a better idea. "Okay, Hailey, I see I'm not going to change your mind." Not tonight, anyway. "Let's call a truce."

She stopped dead in her tracks. "You're giving up?"

"Yeah, I am." He backtracked to her side. "For now."

Seconds of intense staring passed between them. Wolf experienced an uncomfortable pounding in his chest, the one that came every time he looked straight into those gorgeous, heart-stopping green eyes.

"Something tells me you aren't completely giving up on your quest," she said at last.

"A temporary truce is still a truce," he pointed out.

"In other words, I won't be getting rid of you anytime soon."

"That about sums it up."

Her gaze sparkled with a contradictory mix of resignation and…pleasure? Wasn't that interesting?

"Cheer up, sweetheart." Feeling generous, Wolf gave her the big, loopy grin that was guaranteed to make her eyes soften. "All that extra time together could turn out to be a win-win for us both."

Chapter Seven

Wednesday dawned bright and cool. It was another beautiful winter day in southern Georgia. Fort Stewart practically sparkled with sunshine and birdsong.

Far from being deceived by the idyllic scene, Wolf entered his office with a cynical heart. His soldiers weren't adjusting to life in the States as well as he'd hoped. Of course, they'd only been home a week. Maybe they just needed time. And lots of attention from their commanding officer.

Knowing the importance of what lay ahead of him, Wolf tried to keep his mind on work and *not* on Hailey. Not so easy, especially since he'd made a point of staying away from her these last five days.

There was no doubt the woman was unprepared for the hazards of missionary work. But she had to come to that conclusion on her own. With a large nudge from Wolf, of course. The series of survival classes were the perfect vehicle to steer her in the right direction.

In the meantime, Wolf needed to focus on the job the Army paid him to do. First order of business, he needed to decide what to do about the fight he'd just broken up at the PX.

He flexed both his hands in frustration. His unit was already three days into reintegration training, yet the discussions and accompanying videos designed to help soldiers adjust to life back home weren't taking.

Today's fight was not the first Wolf had come across this week. He'd also dealt with a handful of domestic disputes, never a favorite. And some of his soldiers were already showing signs of alcohol abuse. Despite their vehement denials.

Wolf leaned back in his chair and covered his eyes with his hand. There were too many soldiers with too many problems for one man to address, especially a man suffering with his own readjustment issues.

If he was going to have any chance of helping his soldiers, he had to help himself first.

Decision made, he bolted from his chair and headed out of the office without speaking to his NCO.

He'd put off this errand long enough.

Ten minutes later, Wolf sat on the bottom row of bleachers at Cottrell Field and stared at the line of trees across the empty parade grounds. This was the place where soldiers in the Third Infantry Division commemorated the best and worst of Army life.

Alone with his thoughts and far too many emotions churning in his gut, Wolf began to regret his decision to come here today. Terrible memories poked at him.

Refusing to buckle, he rested his forearms on his knees and kept his gaze locked on the long row of evergreens.

His mood threatened to turn dark and turbulent, so he forced his mind back to a happier time, back to the welcome-home ceremony he'd participated in after his first tour of duty. If he closed his eyes he could still hear the music, still feel the energy and sheer joy of being home at last. He'd led his platoon through the tunnel of trees with a large grin on his face. The explosion of cheers from his fellow soldiers' families and friends had made him feel light-headed.

In that one moment, he'd mattered, perhaps for the first time in his life. He was no longer a mistake, as his father had always claimed, no longer the boy unworthy of love, whose own mother had abandoned him at the age of ten. As an officer in the United States Army, Wolf had shed his past and found his future. His life course had been set.

Until the day Clay and the others had died. On his watch.

Struggling to absorb the reality of his failure, Wolf kept his eyes shut and slowed his breathing. In. Out. In. Out. His skin had turned ice-cold, as though there'd been a sudden change in temperature. At least his hands remained steady. He was still in control.

Snapping his eyes open, he stood.

It was time to get this over with.

With slow, determined steps he circled the perimeter of the parade grounds. His boots felt heavier than usual, but he kept moving forward, all the way to the line of trees dedicated to the fallen men and women of the Third ID.

A burst of angry energy slammed into Wolf like a punch. But he didn't stop moving. He tracked slowly down the row, reading each name scrolled on the accompanying plaques.

His steps never faltered until he approached the four shortest trees, the ones representing *his* men. His personal loss.

Images of the bombing besieged him. Flying metal. Stinging flames. His fellow soldiers' screams.

Wolf shuddered. But his eyes remained dry. He was still in control.

Logic told him he wasn't the only one who had missed the signs of the IED. But he'd been the Truck Commander. His sole job had been to hunt for danger.

Fighting back a wave of guilt, he dropped his gaze to the first plaque and read the name aloud. "Staff Sergeant Ronald Matthews."

He moved to the next tree. "Specialist Demitri Ross."

And the next. "Private First Class Kevin Ingram."

At last, he drew alongside the final plaque in the row. "First Lieutenant—" his voice hitched "—Clay O'Brien."

Clay's last words rolled through his mind. *You gotta keep Hailey out of the Sandpit....*

Wolf repeated his response. "I won't let you down."

But what if he did? What if he failed his friend?

No. Unacceptable. Hailey's life depended on Wolf winning their current stalemate.

Desperation made his heartbeat quicken. And then he did something he thought he'd never do again. He lifted up a desperate prayer to God. *Lord, help me stop Hailey from going to the Middle East. Give me the tools and the knowledge to keep her out of harm's way.*

He opened his eyes and studied Clay's tree with an unblinking stare. "Your sister, she's not what I expected.... I don't know...I can't..." His eyes filled with tears.

No. He couldn't do this. Not now. Not today. His control was slipping. He had to get out of here before it vanished completely.

He headed to his car with ground-eating strides.

The sun's ruthless midday rays nearly blinded him,

but not completely, not enough to shield the familiar figure waiting for him at the edge of the field.

"You have a bad habit of turning up at the worst possible moments," Wolf growled through clenched teeth.

"What can I say?" J.T. rolled his shoulders. "It's what I do best."

All kinds of responses came to mind, but Wolf was too drained to verbally spar with the man. "What do you want this time?"

J.T. cocked his head toward the line of trees behind Wolf. "You find Clay's tree?"

"Yeah." Wolf made a sound deep in his throat, half threat, half plea.

"Want to talk about it? It might help to share your burden with someone who's been where you are."

The guy was certainly persistent. "You'll have to excuse me." Wolf pushed past him. "I have to get back to work."

J.T. joined him step for step. "Let me buy you lunch first. Off post. There's a restaurant in Hinesville that serves the best Cuban sandwiches north of Miami."

Wolf increased his pace. "Can't. I have to spend the afternoon scaling a mountain of paperwork."

"One hour won't make a difference."

Wolf hesitated. For a fraction of a second.

J.T. took advantage. "Look, soldier, no agenda here. I just want to go over last-minute details for your class tonight."

Right. Wolf knew what J.T. was doing. The guy was building a relationship with him, instilling trust before he started in with the evangelizing. It's what Wolf would do if their situations were reversed. The realization only managed to aggravate him more. "I'm not one of your mission fields, *Reverend* Wagner."

"Didn't say you were."

Even knowing J.T.'s game, even recognizing what time spent with the man would mean, Wolf relented. "All right. I'll go, but only if you promise me one thing."

"Name it."

"No God talk."

J.T. stopped in front of a black SUV and regarded Wolf with kind, patient eyes. He didn't look like a pastor anymore, but a man who'd been through his own tragedy and was now on the other side. Wolf couldn't help but envy him that.

"I'm not here solely as a pastor."

"Oh, yeah?"

"I figure you need a friend. And maybe—" J.T. drew in a sharp breath "—so do I."

That got Wolf's attention. "Aren't you surrounded by *friends* all day long at your church?"

"You'd be surprised." J.T. unlocked the car door, swung it open but didn't climb in. "People expect a certain…shall we say…behavior out of a pastor. It's hard to be a spiritual leader and human at the same time. Know what I mean?"

Yeah, Wolf knew. As the leader of an entire unit of soldiers he had to keep a professional distance at all times. Consequently, he'd dealt with his share of loneliness through the years. J.T. might be a pastor, but he was proving to be a man with similar challenges as Wolf.

Maybe they could be friends.

Except…

There was something—or rather, *someone*—standing between them. Wolf decided to cut to the chase. "Are you interested in Hailey?"

A rush of emotions fled across J.T.'s face before he covered them with a blank stare. "I'll admit, there was a time when I thought Hailey and I might get together, but it wasn't in God's plan for either of us." He looked expectantly at Wolf, waiting perhaps for him to interrupt.

When he didn't, J.T. continued. "I've long since resigned myself to the fact that she'll never be more than a friend to me." He paused. "What about you? Are you interested in her?"

Despite the fact that Wolf had started this thread, he didn't want to answer the question. What he felt for Hailey was private. Hard to explain. And certainly none of J.T.'s business. But the guy had been candid when he could have hedged. Wolf owed him the same level of honesty. "Yeah. I am."

J.T. went dead still, but Wolf could see the guy's mind working through the new information. Eventually, his face relaxed and he said, "Okay. This is good. No, it's real good. For you both."

Instant relief flooded through Wolf, as if he'd been waiting for J.T.'s blessing. Looked like they were on the road to becoming friends after all.

Thanks to Savannah's notoriously bad traffic, Hailey arrived late to the church Wednesday night. Surprised to see so few empty seats, she slipped along the back row of chairs and sat in one of the last ones available.

Glad the class hadn't started yet, she smiled at several familiar faces. It took her a moment to realize that there was a disproportionate amount of women in the room. Clearly word had spread that a good-looking, *single* Army officer would be teaching the survival classes.

Even as Hailey argued silently with herself, she couldn't stop a possessive thought from taking hold. *Mine.*

Perfect. She was already anxious about seeing

Wolf again. Now she had to contend with a new set of emotions.

The man was quite simply turning her well-planned life into one of uncertainty and raw nerves.

Pulling her bottom lip between her teeth, Hailey gathered her courage and searched for Wolf. She found him standing with J.T. at the front of the room. Heads bent at identical angles, they studied a sheet of paper Wolf held in his hand. So absorbed with the contents on the page, the rest of the room might as well not exist for either man.

Standing shoulder to shoulder, both had an undeniably masculine appeal. Hailey had to admit that J.T. was as good-looking as Wolf. But whenever she thought about pursuing something beyond friendship with the pastor she felt…nothing. Not even a flutter of interest.

But all Wolf had to do was capture her gaze and her stomach performed a somersault.

As though sensing her gaze on him, Wolf lifted his head and scanned the room. When all that intensity leveled onto her, Hailey's stomach began a series of quivering little flips.

She quickly lowered her head and discovered that her fingers were locked in a choke hold around her pen. This crazy reaction to a man she'd known less than a week was absurd.

Relaxing her grip, Hailey looked back up. But Wolf had returned his attention to the paper in his hand.

He still wore his BDUs, the handsome brute. There was something compelling about a man in uniform, especially when the man had broad shoulders, pale blue eyes and day-old stubble running along his jaw. It made a woman think of happily-ever-after and a house full of black-haired children. Dangerous territory for someone who'd lost all of her loved ones to tragedy. Deep down, Hailey couldn't really believe there was a happy ending waiting for her.

She cringed at the thought. But before she could give in to her rising concerns, J.T. walked to the center of the small stage with Wolf following closely behind. They turned to face the room as a unit, looking completely in sync with one another.

Wolf looked at her and winked. *Again* her stomach performed a rolling somersault.

What was she supposed to do with this attraction?

Clay's sage words instantly popped into her mind. *If you're not sure what to do, give it up to God.*

Yes. She would surrender this confusing dilemma to the Lord. Feeling marginally better, Hailey took a calming breath.

J.T. addressed the room. "It's always advisable to go into a foreign country as equipped as possible. Spiritual preparedness is only one of the necessary steps to effective missionary work." He scanned the room with an all-consuming glance. "You should also know how to protect yourself should the worst-case scenario occur."

A few gasps met this remark, but J.T. didn't seem to notice. He motioned Wolf forward. "This is Captain Ty Wolfson, an active-duty soldier who's agreed to teach a six-week course on basic survival skills. I know some of you are heading to Haiti in less than three weeks. We'll make sure you get the bulk of the information you need before you leave. Let's start with a word of prayer."

Everyone in the room bowed their heads, Hailey included.

"Heavenly Father," J.T. began, "I thank you for trusting Your children enough to call us into service. May the world be further evangelized for Your glory, not our own. I pray You open our hearts and minds to what Captain Wolfson has to teach us tonight. We ask all of this in Christ's name. Amen."

Hailey barely had time to raise her head before Wolf took over. "I've had a chance to review a list of all your upcoming mission trips. Since you will be heading into several different locales, I've decided to focus on basic techniques that can be used in any situation or terrain."

He caught Hailey's eye and smiled. He looked entirely too smug, as though he had a secret agenda designed solely for her.

She suppressed a shiver.

"The most important element to survival is between your ears." Wolf pointed to his head to drive home his statement. "If you use your wits and remain calm you'll have a better chance of survival in any situation."

Hailey wrote two things in her notebook: *Stay calm. Use your head.*

Good advice so far, if not a bit obvious.

"Should the worst happen and you end up alone in unknown territory…" Wolf's voice turned grave. "The key is not to panic."

Hailey added to her list. *DON'T PANIC*. She underlined the phrase three times. On the third swipe her hand shook.

"Your priorities should be shelter, water and food, in that order." Wolf strolled through the room as he launched into a description of each category. He meandered down the aisles until he stopped directly in front of Hailey.

Pen poised over her notebook, she gazed up at him.

The look he gave her warned her to brace herself for what was about to come next.

She swallowed.

"Make one mistake and you're in big trouble. Make *two*—" he held the pause for effect "—and you might not survive at all."

Hailey shuddered. Not from the obvious subtext in Wolf's words, but from the intense, almost pleading look in his eyes. He wasn't merely worried about her. He was *afraid* for her.

That undisguised emotion held far more weight than mere words ever could. Wolf knew exactly what life was like in the Middle East. He was making a judgment call on firsthand knowledge. Whereas she was going on an inner tug and a handful of e-mails from Clay before he died.

Horrified to feel a strong thread of doubt take root, Hailey white-knuckled her pen.

Looking a little too pleased with himself, Wolf moved away from her.

As if on cue, J.T. lowered into the empty chair beside her. "Don't let him scare you. He's just trying to make a point."

Hailey lowered her eyes to her notebook. The words *DON'T PANIC* captured her attention. It was an excellent reminder.

"Not to worry," she whispered with renewed resolve. "I'm made of sterner stuff than either of you know."

J.T. patted her hand. "I don't doubt it."

Smiling at her, he rose from his seat and went to lean against his usual spot on the wall a few feet from the door.

Wolf wove his way back to the front of the room. "Over the next six weeks you're going to learn how to signal for help, build a fire, find shelter, gather food and water and administer basic first aid. During our last class together I'll teach you how to protect yourself when attacked, either by a four-legged predator or..." He paused again. "The two-legged kind."

A chorus of gasps wafted through the room. Seemingly oblivious, Wolf punched a button on a laptop and a PowerPoint presentation blinked across the screen behind him.

As he began a detailed instruction on various ways to use a flashlight to signal for help, Hailey's mind raced over his troubling remark about two-legged predators.

Insurgents, terrorists, it didn't matter what name they were called. They were evil men who killed in the name of their god, who cowardly strapped bombs to children and sent them to their deaths.

Am I kidding myself, Lord? Am I trying to change hearts that are unchangeable?

No. She refused to become discouraged. She had a plan, a good one that would involve working directly with Muslim women. Hailey would help educate them and hopefully, in the process, enlighten them to their worth as human beings.

Most of all, she would love them.

It all started with love. Christ's love. And despite Wolf's countless arguments otherwise, Hailey's goal was *not* unattainable. If that were true, Clay died for nothing.

She closed her eyes and tried to picture her brother in her mind. He'd sacrificed his life for his beliefs. She might be called to do the same. Was she ready for that? Was she—

"Hailey?"

She flicked open her eyes and noticed that a shadow had fallen over her paper.

"Hailey."

Heart pounding, she looked up. And straight into Wolf's concerned expression.

"Are you all right?" he asked.

"I was… I mean…" She gave him a shaky smile. "Yes, of course. I'm fine."

The sound of shuffling feet alerted her to a sudden rash of movement coming from all sides of the room. People were getting out of their seats and leaving.

"Where is everyone going?" she asked.

"We're taking a ten-minute break before we meet outside to practice signaling with flashlights."

"Oh." And just like that, her mind went blank. She had nothing else to say. Nada. Zip. Not a single word.

"Come on." He reached out his hand. "If you're especially good, I'll let you be my partner."

Okay, that comment really deserved a response, or maybe even two, and yet words *still* escaped her. Feeling foolish, Hailey silently placed her hand in Wolf's. An immediate sense of well-being filled her.

Right. Now she was tongue-tied for an entirely different set of reasons. Wolf might be a complex, driven, frustrating man, but he was also handsome, charming and appealed to everything female inside her.

Much to Hailey's dismay, and despite J.T.'s raised eyebrows, it felt perfectly natural holding Wolf's hand as they walked out of the room together.

She was still struggling to find her voice when he tugged her down the hallway and toward the back of the church.

Chapter Eight

From the corner of his eye, Wolf watched an array of emotions flutter across Hailey's face. Confusion, sadness, worry, all three were evident in her expression.

"I know what you're trying to do," she said, tilting her chin at the stubborn angle he was growing to dread.

Before responding, he opened the door leading to the empty field behind the church and motioned Hailey to exit ahead of him.

"What is it you think I'm *trying to do?*" he asked.

Nose in the air, she marched several feet forward then spun back to glare at him. "You're trying to scare me." She poked him in the chest. Hard. "Aren't you?"

Denial would be beneath them both. However, there was nothing wrong with a little procrastination. "And if I am?"

"You admit it?"

He took a moment to consider the sky. The night air had turned cold and misty, almost gloomy. Not a single star cut through the thick cloud cover. "Yeah, I admit it." He leaned in close to her ear. "But is it working? Am I scaring you, Hailey?"

A soft, scoffing breath slid past her lips. "Not in the least."

Wolf wasn't fooled by all that false bravado. Like a green soldier on his first deployment, Hailey was scared and riddled with doubts but she didn't know what to do with either emotion.

"Come on, Hailey. I saw the terror in your eyes when I mentioned predators," he said. "We both know I've got you thinking."

"Maybe so." She blinked at him, looking momentarily thrown off guard by the swift admission. "But I am *not* afraid."

"Uh-huh."

"I'm *not*." Her words came out strong enough, but she grabbed his arm as though it had become a lifeline. "I'm just irritated. Yes, that's the word. And maybe a little annoyed at your not-so-subtle attempt to scare me away from my calling."

The look in her eyes said otherwise. "Hailey, there's nothing wrong with being afraid. Fear is good. Fear is healthy. And sometimes—" he looked pointedly at the hand that was now clawing into his biceps "—fear is the only thing that will keep you alive."

"Stop trying to confuse me." Her fingers tightened still more. "Fear is not good. It's the opposite of faith."

"Tell yourself whatever helps you sleep at night. But make no mistake." He slowly unpeeled her hand from his arm, one finger at a time. "I have no intention of watching you climb on an airplane headed to the Middle East. *Ever.*"

Slapping her palm against her thigh, she jerked her chin at him. The building's outdoor lighting gleamed in her eyes, making her look fiercely beautiful and yet painfully vulnerable. He wanted to yank her into his arms and hold her until she wasn't frightened anymore. But that would defeat the purpose of his plan.

So he remained perfectly still and waited for her to break the silence.

"Don't look so smug," she warned. "I *will* get my way on this."

"I'll say the same to you."

She shook her head at him. The building's artificial light turned her dark waves into a rippling black waterfall of curls. She really was extraordinary. She took his breath away.

"So, here we are again. At a stalemate." Her voice rang with such frustration, his chest ached with remorse. He hated being at odds with this woman, even if he was right and she was dead wrong.

"I'm not happy about this, either," he said.

"Then give up. Accept defeat."

"Not a chance." Despite her arguments otherwise, he'd won this round. Hailey was having doubts, just as he planned.

Next order of business. Wolf needed to reveal the harsh realities of the Sandpit. In living color. The most accessible footage was on the Internet.

But how was he going to get the stubborn woman in front of a computer?

While he was contemplating various possibilities, she changed the subject on him. "How are you settling into life back in the States?"

"Slowly." He wondered if he should tell her about his visit to Cottrell Field this morning but quickly decided against it. There was already too much tension between them. He didn't want Clay in the middle, too. "I'm moving off post this weekend."

"But…" Her eyebrows slammed together. "I didn't realize you were living there."

"Only temporarily. I'm moving to a town house in Savannah." As soon as the words left his mouth he had his idea. "Would you help me shop for towels, kitchenware, you know, stuff like that? I could use a woman's opinion."

Especially if that woman was the green-eyed beauty staring at him now. He watched in fascination as Hailey transitioned right before his eyes from a woman of fierce resolve to one filled with age-old female secrets. The kind that hooked a man into all sorts of promises.

"Of course I'll help you," she all but purred. A slow grin spread across her face. "Under one condition."

His blood pumped slow and thick through his veins. Oh, yeah. He'd give this woman anything she asked of him. *"Anything."*

"I want a ride on your motorcycle." She raised her hand to keep him from speaking over her. "Or no deal."

He couldn't resist a smile at the sight of all that fierce determination. "Done."

Really, that had to be the easiest bargain he'd ever struck with another human being.

Saturday morning dawned clear, the blue sky completely cloudless. Hailey, however, had several other concerns on her mind that wiped out her joy over the gorgeous weather.

Frowning, she climbed out of Wolf's car and jammed her fists on her hips. "It's not that I don't appreciate Stella." She eyed the steel monster for a long moment, her annoyance melting into an odd sort of fondness. "In fact, the old girl's starting to grow on me."

"She does have her charm," Wolf agreed, patting the roof of the car with a rather unhealthy dose of affection.

What is it with him and this car? And why did it matter to Hailey so much? She couldn't possibly be jealous of a hunk of metal.

Could she?

"Nevertheless," she said, sharply ignoring the knot of unease twisting in her stomach. "I find it necessary to remind you that we had a deal. You promised me a ride on your motorcycle before we went shopping. And yet, here we are."

She made a grand sweep of her hand, making sure the arc included not only the building but the entire parking lot.

Laughing softly, he swung his arm over her shoulder and tugged her against his warm, muscular body. "Come on, Hail, lighten up. You know we can't cart around supplies on my bike."

She answered with a very unladylike snort.

"Tell you what." He drew her in a fraction closer to his chest. "You fulfill your end of the bargain and as soon as we're done here I'll fulfill mine."

Instead of shoving him away—like she should, considering his arrogant tone—Hailey snuggled deeper inside Wolf's embrace. She told herself this strange desire to be near him had nothing, *nothing,* to do with the sense of comfort and safety she felt in his arms. Nor was it because of the pleasant tingle running up her spine that came when she breathed in his masculine scent of leather, soap and spice.

No. The decision to cling to him was all about the cool breeze sweeping across the parking lot. Nothing more.

Then why did she feel so lost when he dropped his

arm and headed toward the store's entrance ahead of her?

"So, uh, Wolf." Hailey trotted after him. "Remind me again why we're shopping here and not on post."

"Simple." He pulled loose a shopping cart from the long stack, his gaze riveted on a colorful display of a popular sports drink. "More variety."

"But everything's so much more expensive here," she said.

He went completely still at her remark. The only part of him moving was his blinking eyelashes.

"Wolf?"

"I can afford this store," he ground out through a clenched jaw.

Momentarily bemused by the sudden change in him, Hailey looked everywhere but at his irritated expression. How could she have predicted he'd be so touchy? Because Clay had been the same way when he'd first returned from Iraq. Seemingly inconsequential things had upset him, while others had not. There had been no predicting his reaction, not at first, not until he'd acclimated.

"Wolf, I'm sorry," she began carefully. "I didn't mean to imply that you couldn't afford this store. I was only trying to be practical. I…" She sighed. "I apologize."

He responded with a distant nod. "Okay."

It wasn't much of an acceptance. Probably because her apology hadn't sounded sincere enough. "Really, Wolf. I'm sorry."

"I know." He pushed the cart out of the way of oncoming traffic. "Try to understand, Hailey. To me, shopping in *any* store is a luxury. After a year in the desert, I just want to cruise aisles full of so many choices my head spins. And this particular store is known for its variety."

"Then what are we waiting for? Let's get to it."

They shopped for two full hours, wading up and down the aisles with no real plan. Understanding the situation better, Hailey allowed Wolf to push the cart at his pace. She also stood by patiently while he struggled over what seemed basic, straightforward decisions to her.

To him, they were dilemmas.

What color towels should he pick? Did he need four dinner plates or eight? Two skillets or one?

She could tell by the increasingly taut series of expressions on his face that each decision was getting harder for him to make.

They turned onto the small appliance aisle, and he stopped. He just stopped. Right there. In the middle of the aisle, and stood motionless, blinking rapidly, seemingly riveted by whatever he saw up ahead of him.

Desperation suddenly filled his gaze. And then...

His eyes went dead.

Hailey had lost him. Completely. And she wasn't sure how to get him back.

An ugly void of nothing filled Wolf's mind, followed by an intense rush of panic. Rage hovered so close to the edge of his control he didn't know what to do with it.

His thoughts tumbled over one another so quickly he had to grip the shopping cart ruthlessly to keep his hands from shaking.

There were too many noises surrounding him, too many colors and too many people. So...many... people.

He was having sensory overload. He recognized the signs, yet he was too detached from himself to do anything about it.

He couldn't make another decision. Not. One. More. But that wasn't the main reason his mind had become a ball of chaotic fury.

It was the ridiculous argument he'd overheard. The one still going on behind him.

He breathed in a slow, careful breath, then let it out even slower. But nothing helped. His anger increased as the woman carried on, complaining about the low thread count in the bedsheets someone had handed her. On and on she went.

Didn't she understand what a privilege it was to purchase a set of bedsheets in the first place? Didn't she know how fortunate she was to have a bed at all, much less sheets and blankets? And yet she was *still* complaining.

Wolf had to get out of here. Before he said—or did—something he couldn't take back.

"Wolf." Hailey's voice called to him from what seemed a great distance. He'd nearly forgotten she was here with him.

She placed a gentle hand on his arm. The soft touch instantly calmed him.

"Wolf, honey." Her voice washed over him in soothing ripples. "Look at me."

He rolled his gaze in her direction.

They stared at one another, both understanding that he was teetering on the edge.

"Why don't you wait for me in the car?" she suggested softly.

He shook his head, unable to focus completely on

what she was saying, but knowing he needed to do what she advised.

"Go on." She nudged him with her hip. "I'll finish up here."

"I—"

"It's all right." She cupped his cheek tenderly. "Just go to the car. I've got this."

He resisted the urge to close his eyes and lean into her hand. "I need air," he admitted.

"Oh, Wolf, it's okay." She caressed his cheek. "It's *okay*."

Her kindness—he didn't know what to do with it. Part of him wanted to embrace it, to fall into all that goodness and affection he saw in her eyes. Another part of him wanted to run because he couldn't release the anger gnawing at him.

Lash out? Escape? Both viable options. Which meant he had a classic case of fight or flight.

Without another word he turned on his heel and started toward the front of the store. He halted after two steps.

His breathing wouldn't stop its erratic rhythm, his head swam with too many angry images but at least he had the presence of mind to remember where he was, who he was with and what they were doing.

"Here." He dug his wallet out of his back pocket and handed her a bunch of bills. "Use the cash to pay for my purchases."

She took the money without question. "I'll make this quick."

"Okay."

"Go on, Wolf. It's all right." Her eyes held such understanding, it made him feel stripped to the bone. He didn't want anyone, not even Hailey, to see that deeply into his soul.

He stalked to the store's entrance at a fast pace. His chest ached. His eyes burned. But he kept his mind blank and his senses shut down, refusing to look at people, or listen to any more of their conversations.

He'd never felt this before, this all-consuming fury.

But he'd never felt this alone before, either.

Not even in those early days after his father died of alcohol poisoning. Although Wolf had been saddened by the tragic passing, there had also been a sense of relief. His father had been set free from his pain. Wolf had turned to God after that, and had discovered that his faith could get him through the worst life tossed his way.

He had never wavered in his beliefs. Until his Humvee had hit the IED.

Wolf's steps grew heavy, but he made it to Stella and planted his palm on the car's hood. Breathing slowly, methodically, he lifted his eyes to heaven. *Lord, I need Your help. I need…*

What? What did he want from a God that had abandoned him on that Iraqi roadside?

As soon as the question materialized Wolf knew. He wanted his faith back. He wanted to believe again. He wanted God to prove to him he wasn't here by mistake. That he still mattered.

And that maybe, just maybe, he was worthy of a woman like Hailey O'Brien.

Gulping for air, Wolf climbed into the car and sat behind the driver's seat. He leaned on the steering wheel and cradled his head on his forearms.

Dear Lord, I…

He didn't know what to pray for first, there were so

many requests running through his mind. He knew he wanted to find a purpose beyond himself, something that meant he was more than just a guy who'd randomly survived an IED attack, while better men had died.

But, wait, he already had such a purpose. He already had a worthy goal.

At last, he knew what to pray. "Lord, I need Your help with Hailey. I need Your guidance. But if You remain silent, if You refuse Your assistance, I will stop her from her dangerous quest somehow. I *will* find a way."

No matter the cost.

Get 2 Books FREE!

Love Inspired Books,
publisher of inspirational fiction,
presents

Love Inspired

A series of contemporary love stories that will lift your spirits and reinforce important lessons about life, faith and love!

FREE BOOKS! Use the reply card inside to get two free books by outstanding inspirational authors!

FREE GIFTS! You'll also get two exciting surprise gifts, absolutely free!

GET 2 BOOKS

IF YOU ENJOY A ROMANTIC STORY that reflects solid, traditional values, then you'll like *Love Inspired*® novels. These are heartwarming inspirational romances that explore timeless themes of forgiveness and redemption, sacrifice and spiritual fulfillment.

We'd like to send you two *Love Inspired* novels absolutely free. Accepting them puts you under no obligation to purchase any more books.

HOW TO GET YOUR
2 FREE BOOKS AND 2 FREE GIFTS

1. Return the reply card today, and we'll send you two *Love Inspired* novels, absolutely free! We'll even pay the postage!

2. Accepting free books places you under no obligation to buy anything, ever. The two books have combined cover prices of at least $11.00 in the U.S. and at least $13.00 in Canada, but they're yours to keep, free!

3. We hope that after receiving your free books you'll want to remain a subscriber, but the choice is yours—to continue or cancel, any time at all!

EXTRA BONUS

You'll also get two free mystery gifts! (worth about $10)

FREE!

Return this card promptly to get
2 FREE BOOKS and 2 FREE GIFTS!

YES! Please send me 2 FREE *Love Inspired*® novels, and 2 free mystery gifts as well. I understand I am under no obligation to purchase anything, as explained on the back of this insert.

About how many NEW paperback fiction books have you purchased in the past 3 months?

❑ 0-2   ❑ 3-6   ❑ 7 or more
E5TW   E5T9   E5JM

❑ I prefer the regular-print edition   ❑ I prefer the larger-print edition
105/305 IDL   **122/322 IDL**

Please Print

FIRST NAME

LAST NAME

ADDRESS

APT.#   CITY

Visit us at
www.ReaderService.com

STATE/PROV.   ZIP/POSTAL CODE

▲ If offer card is missing write to: The Reader Service, P.O. Box 1867, Buffalo, NY 14240-1867 or visit www.ReaderService.com ▲

BUSINESS REPLY MAIL

FIRST-CLASS MAIL   PERMIT NO. 717   BUFFALO, NY

POSTAGE WILL BE PAID BY ADDRESSEE

THE READER SERVICE
PO BOX 1867
BUFFALO NY 14240-9952

NO POSTAGE
NECESSARY
IF MAILED
IN THE
UNITED STATES

Chapter Nine

Hailey found Wolf sitting alone in his car. He leaned heavily on the steering wheel, with one foot resting on Stella's floorboard and the other flat on the concrete. He hadn't noticed Hailey yet, probably because he was looking straight ahead, his eyes glazed and unfocused.

All that masculine vulnerability radiating out of him took her breath away. Tears leaked out of her eyes. She brushed them away with a quick swipe. It was so easy to forget this big, charming man had just returned from a war zone where he'd lost four of his men, including his best friend.

Searching for the right words, Hailey wheeled the overflowing shopping cart out of the way of traffic and stopped next to him.

"Wolf?"

He blinked once, twice, then swung around to face her.

The war of emotions raging in his gaze evened out at last and his expression cleared.

Wolf was back.

Heaving a sigh of relief, Hailey crouched down in

front of him. "I was worried about you," she whispered, afraid to say the words too loudly.

He placed his hands on her shoulders and something moved inside her, something good and permanent and *terrifying*. She was falling for this gorgeous, sad, courageous man, and she wasn't sure what came next.

Wolf's gaze softened. "Thank you, Hailey."

"For...for what?"

"For knowing what to do back there. For getting me out of the store before something bad happened. No one has ever cared about me like that." His blue eyes flickered with gratitude. "I owe you. I—"

He broke off, blinked. Blinked again. He had more to say. She saw it in the way the muscles jumped in his jaw, but then his gaze filled with a different sort of intent and he leaned forward.

Hailey's stomach dropped to her toes at the same moment Wolf's mouth pressed lightly against hers.

He was actually kissing her. Right there, in the middle of the busiest parking lot in Savannah. And...and...*she* was kissing him back. Rather enthusiastically, if she did say so herself.

Surprised at her behavior, Hailey lost her balance. Wolf caught her with a hand behind her back, the movement enough to break the kiss.

He smiled slowly and her stomach performed a perfect roll.

"Well," he said, still grinning.

"Well," she repeated.

"I didn't plan that."

"I...I know." She angled her head slightly away. This good-looking, flawed soldier had too much power over her, enough to make her start building dreams of happily-ever-after around him.

Was that why he'd kissed her? Had it all been part of his plan? To distract her from her goal?

"This doesn't change anything," she said with only a hint of her usual conviction. "I'm still going to the Middle East."

He knuckled a lock of her hair off her face. "I'd be disappointed if a simple kiss could change your mind that easily."

Simple? Who was he kidding? There was nothing *simple* about that kiss, and they both knew it.

"Of course." He twirled the errant strand around his finger. "I think it's only fair to warn you that I'm still going to do everything in my power to sway you to my way of thinking."

"I'd be disappointed if a simple kiss could change your mind that easily," she said, using his own words against him.

He laughed, a quick burst of humor. Finally, he looked like his old self again, enough that internal warning bells sounded the alarm in Hailey's head. "We have a lot of bags to unload," she reminded them both. "We should probably get to it."

He looked over her shoulder and grimaced. "Right." He helped her stand. "Come on. We're burning daylight."

Working in silence, they stashed the bags in the trunk. Ever the gentleman, Wolf helped Hailey into her seat before heading to his side of the car.

While he rounded the front end, she debated whether or not to bring up the incident in the store. Over the last week, she'd done considerable research about returning war veterans and their unique struggles. Wolf had some clear signs of battle fatigue, but not all of them.

According to one article, too many people pretended

nothing was wrong. But silence was often the biggest detriment to a soldier's healing. If Wolf was going to overcome whatever was bothering him, he *had* to talk about it.

Sorting through several different approaches to the conversation, Hailey waited until he shut the car door and turned to look at her. "Ready?"

She shook her head. "No. First, I'd like you to tell me what happened back there."

"We, uh—" he looked quickly away "—kissed?"

Yes. Oh, *yes,* they had. But that wasn't what she meant. "Lovely as it was, I'm not talking about our kiss."

"You thought it was...*lovely?*" He didn't seem to know what to make of that.

"No, actually, I thought it was spectacular."

"Yeah." A very masculine grin spread across his lips. "It was."

Refusing to let him sidetrack her—which, unfortunately, he was on the verge of doing—Hailey refocused the conversation. "I was talking about what happened in the store."

His smile vanished, but he didn't seem as disturbed by the question as she would have expected. In fact, he looked like he wanted to talk. Which, according to Hailey's research, was a really, *really* good sign.

She relaxed back against her seat in relief, until she realized he wasn't actually talking. Not yet, anyway.

Perhaps he didn't know where to start.

She decided to help him out. "Were there too many choices in there? Was that what triggered your, um... reaction?"

His lips twisted into a frown. "Not exactly. It was that ridiculous argument I overheard."

"What argument?" she asked, more than a little confused.

"There was a woman, just behind us, or maybe one aisle over, complaining about the low thread count on the sheets." He shook his head in disgust. "She was making it sound like it was the end of the world because she couldn't find sheets soft enough for her guest room."

Hailey furrowed her brow. Why would something so innocuous shove him close to the edge? "I'm not sure I understand."

Wolf's eyes took on a hard expression. "There was such entitlement in her tone, like it was her *right* to have the softest sheets known to man, when so many people in the world don't even have a bed."

His words triggered a surprisingly strong reaction in Hailey, a mixture of shame and guilt and conviction. Her greatest fear was that she'd end up like that woman, ungrateful for the advantages in her life.

"I know I overreacted," Wolf admitted. "It's not that I begrudge people having nice things. That's what makes this country great. You know? The freedom to choose, to achieve, to go after whatever we want, whether it's good for us or not."

Finally, Hailey understood what had happened to Wolf inside the store. "You want people in this country to appreciate what we have," she ventured. "That's what got you so upset, the woman's lack of gratitude."

He shrugged. "My anger was out of proportion to the situation. I've never been that furious in my life. Not even when my mother walked out and left me to care for my alcoholic father all by myself."

What? His mother had abandoned him? Hailey forgot all about soft sheets and sufficient gratitude. It took all her mental effort to fight off the powerful rush of anger slamming through her. The emotion was so strong she could hardly breathe.

"How old were you when she left?" she asked, her voice sounding oddly calm, considering the fury building inside her.

"Ten."

So young? "Oh, Wolf, how awful."

He looked at her oddly. "Didn't you say Clay told you about me?"

She nodded, unsure why he'd steered the conversation in that direction.

"Clay never told you about my childhood?"

"Of course not," she assured him. "He wouldn't have betrayed your confidence like that."

Instead of offering comfort, her words seemed to make him tenser. "I don't understand what you mean."

There was so much confusion in him. Didn't he realize how loyal Clay had been to their friendship? "The circumstance of your childhood wasn't Clay's secret to tell, not even to me. He kept his descriptions to your character and how it showed in everyday, ordinary events."

Like how Wolf always had time to play soccer with the local Iraqi kids, even when he was exhausted from a full day's grueling work. How he accepted the dangerous missions others didn't want to take. How he would speak with his soldiers, whenever, wherever, no matter the situation or problem.

So caught up in trying to remember the rest of what Clay had said, Hailey barely noticed Wolf shutting down again. With very controlled movements, he slipped on his sunglasses and reached for the ignition.

"Wait." She placed her hand over his. "Did you say

you had to take care of your alcoholic father? All by yourself?"

He let go of the key and sat back. "You caught that, huh?"

"But you were only ten years old." A baby, really. At that age she'd had nothing more on her mind than dance classes, swimming lessons and what candy to pick at the movies.

"I grew up fast," he said.

And suffered for it, she thought, in ways she couldn't possibly understand. A child should never have to be that responsible at such a young age. "I can't imagine how hard it must have been for you."

"You have no idea." He ran his fingertip along the steering wheel, round and round and round. "My father was a mean drunk."

Hailey hurt for the little boy he'd once been. So much her heart ached. Not only had he been forced to become an adult at the age of ten, he'd clearly been wounded by the two people he was supposed to rely on most, his parents. Yet, despite all his hardships, Wolf had turned out to be an exceptional leader, a man others trusted with their lives.

Clay had said Wolf was the best person he knew. Hailey completely agreed.

Tentatively, she reached out and touched his hand. When he didn't pull away, she curled her fingers around his.

He stared at their joined hands for a long moment. "The Army is the only real family I've ever known. But now, after the bombing—" he swallowed hard "—even that's tainted."

Unable to stop herself, Hailey pressed a tender kiss to his cheek, then fell back in her seat once again.

He touched the place where she'd kissed him, smiled briefly then dropped his hand and scowled again. "I go over the details of that day in my head, over and over again, wondering how I missed the signs of the IED."

Hailey's eyes widened at the self-recrimination in his voice. "You don't actually believe the accident was your fault?"

"Maybe I do." His words came out barely audible.

What a terrible, terrible burden to carry all these months. "Were you driving?" she asked. "Is that why you think you're to blame?"

"No." He shook his head. "Clay was behind the wheel. Like always. But, Hailey, I was the Truck Commander." He looked at her with genuine remorse in his eyes. "It was my job to be on the lookout for trouble."

She supposed that argument made an odd sort of sense—to him. But it wasn't the full story. It couldn't be. He was leaving too much out. Nothing in life was ever that black-and-white.

"If my brother was driving, like you said, doesn't that mean he missed the bomb, too? And what about the gunner?" She pictured in her mind the Humvee Clay had once shown her. "If he was standing in the turret, wouldn't he have had a fuller range of vision than either you or Clay?"

"We all missed the bomb," Wolf said quietly. "But it was my sole responsibility to see it in time."

Knowing exactly what to say, Hailey touched his shoulder. "Wolf. I don't blame you for Clay's death."

The muscles beneath her hand tensed. "Because of my negligence four good men are dead, including your brother. I stole your family from you, all because I missed something I was trained to see."

The despair in Wolf's voice shook her to the core.

Now she understood why he was so determined to follow through with his promise to Clay.

"The explosion was not your fault," she insisted, gripping his shoulder in earnest. "If you need someone to blame, blame the insurgents who laid the bomb. Blame the terrorists who hate us so much they fight dirty. They are the ones who stole Clay from us. And, yes, Wolf." She leaned closer to him. "Make no mistake. We both lost our brother that day."

Making a strangled sound deep in his throat, Wolf pulled away from her and reached for the ignition again. One twist of his wrist and Stella exploded into action.

Hailey jumped back at the awful sound. Even if she wanted to continue the conversation, Wolf wouldn't be able to hear her over the roar of the engine.

What a convenient way to end the conversation.

Only after he put the car in gear did Stella's obnoxious growl settle into a loud purr.

"Once we unpack the supplies," Wolf said over the rumble, "I have a video I need to show you on my computer."

Considering the grim twist of Wolf's lips and his cold, intimidating tone, Hailey knew she didn't want to see whatever was on that video.

But she would sit through the show, for no other reason than to prove to Wolf she didn't blame him for Clay's death. Then, *maybe,* he would stop holding himself responsible, as well.

The unpacking and subsequent organizing took longer than Wolf anticipated. The sun had gone down a full hour ago. With it, the temperature had dropped at least ten more degrees. Wolf's leg ached like an angry bear.

Rubbing out a kink in his thigh, he looked over

at Hailey puttering around in his kitchen. The mood had lightened between them, enough that he no longer wanted to talk—or even think—about what had happened in Iraq. He just wanted to enjoy her company.

He watched, fascinated, as she went to the sink and flipped on the faucet. After squirting dish soap in the pooling water, she tackled the task of washing a stack of plates recently freed from their packaging.

Unable to take his eyes off her, Wolf's heart took a tumble in his chest. Hailey moved with a sleek grace that captivated him. She was all poise and fluid motion and beneath her deceptively easygoing manner was the heart of a warrior. She would fight for her beliefs to the bitter end. He'd been kidding himself to think otherwise. She would also stand boldly beside those she considered her own.

Wolf wanted to be hers.

Taking a deep breath, he rocked back on his heels and tried not to disturb her while he was battling this strange mood.

Then again, why not interrupt her?

Decision made, he ambled into the kitchen.

"Are you planning to work through dinner?" he asked in what he hoped was a light tone. He couldn't tell over the drumming of his pulse in his ears.

She looked over her shoulder and smiled. "What time is it?"

Captured in that sweet gaze, he swallowed. "Just after eight."

"I didn't realize it was so late." She looked around the town house and her smile deepened. "We've certainly accomplished a lot."

"Enough for one day." He concentrated on a spot over her head, searching for anything to keep his mind off the way his heartbeat continued to pick up speed at an alarming rate. "Let's get something to eat."

"But I'm not through washing dishes."

"I say you are."

He reached around her, turned off the faucet then stepped back. She spun around with a gasp. Blinking rapidly, she looked flustered and confused and adorable. He had to fight not to pull her into his arms and kiss her.

There was something about this woman that called to the man in him. He felt incredibly normal around her. And accepted, truly accepted.

A flood of warmth captured his cold heart. Hailey O'Brien was a special woman. By refusing to hold him responsible for her brother's death, she made him want to forgive himself, to turn back to God and be a better man, the man he never thought he could be but desperately wanted to become.

She moved a step closer, piercing him with her gaze. There was curiosity in her eyes. And something else. Something that told him she was fully aware of him, fully engaged in the moment.

Needing something to do, Wolf grabbed a dish towel off the counter, took her hands in his and began drying them.

She let out a shaky sigh.

He liked that sound. It made him feel like an alpha male, called to protect his woman from danger. And, yeah, Hailey was starting to feel like his woman.

"Are you going to kiss me again?" she asked with unmistakable excitement in her eyes.

He could get used to her looking at him like that. Grinning like the Big, Bad Wolf she'd once called him, he continued rubbing her hands. Slowly. Methodically. "It's a high possibility."

"So, um…" She cleared her throat. "Are you going to do it anytime soon?"

He tossed the towel over his shoulder, then lifted one of her hands to his lips. "I'm thinking about it."

Now she looked annoyed and maybe a little impatient. "Are you gonna think about it much longer?"

"That bother you?" he asked, knowing full well that it did.

"You bet it does." She tugged her hands free and then skimmed her fingertips across his cheek. "You have exactly five seconds to get busy, soldier. Or I'll take matters into my own hands."

He liked that idea. A lot. "How long do I have left?"

"About three seconds."

"One…" He counted slowly, fighting for patience. "Two…"

She let out a feminine huff and grabbed his shoulders. "Three."

He closed his eyes as she pressed her lips to his. Her kiss was tentative, innocent and so sweet Wolf's eyes stung behind his lids.

Just as he started enjoying himself, she pulled her head back. "There." Her tone rang with triumph.

Wolf grinned at her, realizing he hadn't felt this good in a long time. Maybe never. "Very nice."

A blush spread across her cheeks.

He leaned forward for another kiss, but then her stomach growled and he stopped his pursuit. "Hungry much?"

She gave him a wry grin. "I suppose I should warn you. I get mean when I don't eat."

He doubted that, but he played along. "Then we better get you fed." He walked over to the counter and yanked Stella's keys into his hand. "If I remember correctly, you owe me a pizza."

"I'll gladly pay up." She took the keys out of his hand and twirled them around her index finger. "But before we head out, didn't you want to show me something on your computer first?"

His good mood plummeted at the reminder. With considerable effort, he folded his emotions further inside him and took his keys back. Nothing was going to ruin this moment, especially not a series of video clips of IED explosions. "Later. Maybe after we eat."

Thankfully, she didn't argue. "Okay."

Wolf watched, mesmerized, as she twisted her hair into one of those intricate braids only women knew how to build.

"What are you doing?" he asked.

"I'm pulling my hair back so it'll fit under the helmet."

"What helmet?"

She gave him a pitying look. "The one I have to wear to ride on your motorcycle."

He shook the car keys in front of her nose. "We're taking Stella."

"Oh, no. No, no." She plucked the keys back and then tossed them into the sink of soapy water. "You promised me a ride on your motorcycle."

Wolf was already shaking his head before she finished speaking. No way was he putting her on his bike at this hour. "It's too dark outside."

"Why would riding in the dark be a problem?" She angled her head at him. "Don't you have a headlight?"

"Sure, but you won't be able to see much. Why bother?"

"Because I'll be able to tap into my other senses. Feel the wind on my face. Hear the roar of the traffic. Maybe smell the pine trees. As a matter of fact…" She drummed a finger on her chin. "Not being able to see just might make the whole experience more exciting."

It probably would, Wolf silently admitted to himself. But he wasn't giving in to her request. Riding a cycle could be dangerous. Riding at night even more so.

"Come on, Wolf."

"Absolutely not."

She gave him a sad puppy-dog look that just about broke his heart. "Please?"

"No."

"I have tricks to make you change your mind."

Okay, that sounded interesting. "Yeah? Like what?"

She opened her mouth, shut it, concentrated for a moment, then began again. "You might as well quit arguing. You will give in."

In the face of all that female confidence, Wolf knew she was right. She was going to win this one. But his pride wouldn't allow him to go down without a fight. The woman was going to have to earn her ride.

"Go ahead, sweetheart." He folded his arms across his chest. "Convince me."

Chapter Ten

Smiling in triumph, Hailey wrapped her arms around Wolf's waist and prepared to enjoy the ride. She couldn't hear much over the noise of the motorcycle's engine.

She didn't care.

She felt great. Free. And to think, she'd nearly missed out on this fabulous experience because of Wolf's stubbornness.

Thankfully, he'd given in to her request. All it had taken was a few steps in his direction, a lot of female attitude on her part and a saucy grin. The poor man had gone down without a fight.

But right now, instead of gloating—there'd be plenty of time for that—Hailey allowed herself to embrace all the wonderful sensations of the moment.

Her pulse raced in time with the roar of the engine. Her stomach flipped over and over and over again. While her eyes filled with happy tears.

This was an adventure she wouldn't soon forget.

No denying it, Hailey had lived a sheltered life. If she'd have continued existing in her safe, predictable world, she'd have missed out on today. She'd have missed out on Wolf.

Smiling broadly, she hugged him a little tighter.

Misunderstanding the gesture, he slowed down. "Sorry," he yelled over the wind. "Didn't mean to scare you."

Touched that he was that concerned about her, she shouted back, "I'm not afraid."

"Really?"

She laughed into the wind. "Speed up."

With a twist of his wrist, he did as she requested, muttering something that sounded suspiciously like, "Woman after my own heart."

Hailey sighed, ready to admit the truth at last. She wasn't falling for Wolf, she'd already fallen. It had been coming on for a while, maybe all the way back to Clay's first e-mails about his friend with the odd nickname. In some place deep within her, Hailey had been waiting for Wolf to come home to her.

And now that he was here, she was a better person for knowing him. It wasn't just his good looks that had captured her heart. It was his courage. His integrity. And, oddly enough, his devotion to her brother's last request.

Not that he'd win that particular argument, but Wolf's commitment to his promise showed what sort of man he was deep at his core.

With another twist of his wrist, he slowed the motorcycle so he could take the off-ramp that fed into Savannah's historic district.

The moment they turned onto Liberty, Hailey sighed. Her ride was drawing to an end.

Traffic was light at this time of year. That didn't mean there weren't tourists. They passed three separate walking tours in less than five city blocks.

Determined to squeeze every ounce of pleasure out

of this adventure, Hailey tried to look at the downtown from a visitor's perspective. She knew the draw was the city's rich history and unique architecture. But to her, Savannah was simply home. The only one she'd ever known.

She would miss living here when she left for the Middle East. The city had a quirkiness and charm that couldn't be found in any other place in the world. Once she became a full-time missionary, Hailey would have to leave everything and everyone she loved behind.

She fought back a frown, but couldn't stop the wave of sadness that coursed through her veins.

Wolf pulled the motorcycle to a stop in front of her house and her mood took another turn for the worse. Feeling apprehensive, she climbed off the bike and then yanked off her helmet with a little more force than necessary.

"Why don't you come inside," she said, eyeing Wolf carefully. "Once we order the pizza I'll grab my laptop and you can cue up whatever it was you wanted to show me."

Wolf looked up at her house. A shadow of unease crossed his face, but then he gave one firm nod of agreement. "Yeah, okay. It might be better to do this here. Where you're comfortable."

At his businesslike manner a shiver of foreboding passed through her. Worse, the tension was back between them. Suspecting what he planned to show her, Hailey doubted the evening would end on a high note. And that was the real shame here.

Sitting alone at Hailey's kitchen table, Wolf waited for her to return with her laptop. His hunger had all but disappeared. And with each passing second, his doubts increased.

Maybe this wasn't the best time to show Hailey the video montage he'd found on the Internet. When the idea had first occurred to him, his primary goal had been to scare her into staying home.

Now, he wasn't sure he wanted to frighten her. Not like this. But how else could he convince her of the dangers she would face in the Middle East? Reason hadn't worked. So far the survival classes hadn't done the trick. Even his well-thought-out pleas had fallen on deaf ears.

Wolf was out of ideas.

So here he sat, rubbing his aching leg, preparing to fight dirty. But what else could he do? Walk away? Not going to happen.

He tapped his knee with an impatient drumming of his fingers, wishing Hailey would return soon. The picture of her and Clay still hung on her refrigerator. The sight of all that happiness, now lost forever, was a bold reminder of why Wolf had to resort to shock tactics in order to bring Hailey into compliance with her brother's wishes.

Glancing at the photograph, it struck him once again just how different the tuxedoed Clay was from the fearless soldier Wolf remembered. The guy in the picture looked younger, more carefree, on the brink of continuing the O'Brien legacy.

Hailey looked equally charmed and ready to take her place in the world, as well. In that brief snapshot in time, the future was full of possibilities for them both.

Then Clay had gone off to war. And everything had changed.

Guilt weighed like a stone in Wolf's gut. Had Clay

survived the IED instead of him, would he be the one sitting in this kitchen waiting for his sister to return? Perhaps they'd be planning Clay's next career move, Hailey's unconditional support making the choices seem endless.

What would it be like to have that kind of woman in his life, a woman who knew what loyalty and permanence meant?

Wolf had no answer to the question. The mere suggestion was beyond his comprehension. How could a man whose own mother hadn't wanted him ever understand a woman like Hailey and what it would take to make her happy?

Before he could ponder the question, Hailey returned and joined him at the table.

"We have at least thirty minutes before the pizza arrives." She slid a high-end laptop computer toward him. "It's booted up. What did you want to show me?"

Against his better judgment, Wolf held Hailey's gaze a moment too long. She wasn't exactly scowling, but her eyes were bright and full of apprehension, as though she sensed what was about to come. With all that emotion brimming in her gaze, she looked far too young to head into a war zone.

If the insurgents got hold of her, they would...they would...

Wolf shook the thought away with a fierce jerk of his head.

He hated what he was about to do, but he hated the idea of this beautiful, untouched woman heading into danger even more.

He swallowed back the last of his misgivings and lowered his gaze to the computer.

A few keystrokes later he found the Web site he wanted. Two more clicks and the video montage was ready to go.

"Okay. We're all set." He glanced over at Hailey again. "I'm going to show you a few scenarios similar to the one where your brother died."

"Wolf, no." Panic filled her gaze. "I don't need to see how Clay died. He's with the Lord now, and that's all that matters. It's not important how he got there."

"Unfortunately, how he died *is* important." Wolf covered her hand with his. The idea of losing her to the violence of the Middle East was enough to steal his breath. "I'm sorry, Hailey, I can't let either of us forget why I sought you out in the first place."

She squeezed her eyes shut, took a deep breath and then slowly nodded. "Okay, fine. Let's just get this over with."

"It's for the best," he said, trying to convince himself as much as her.

But for the first time since Clay's death, Wolf felt the stirrings of genuine anger. Not guilt but anger, bordering on fury. Why had his friend put him in this impossible situation?

If Wolf kept Hailey out of the Middle East, she could easily end up bitter, perhaps never forgiving him for taking away her dream, as misguided as it was. On the other hand, if she did make it to the Sandpit, she could just as easily lose her life to a random act of violence. Or worse.

As bad as either scenario was, Wolf knew his duty.

With a surprisingly steady hand, he pressed the Enter key. An image from a homemade video filled the screen.

No turning back now.

* * *

Hailey held her breath as Wolf swung the computer to face her again. She braced against the emotions bubbling inside her, with little success.

Relax, relax, relax, she told herself, but she couldn't hold back the sick feeling of panic whirling in her stomach.

Wolf wasn't playing fairly.

Nevertheless, Hailey would endure this terrible moment. And then she would get through the next. And then the next, holding steady through the entire process until Wolf shut off the computer.

Blinking hard, she took in the scene playing out on the screen. A soft gasp flew from her lips.

The video Wolf had cued up had been taken from atop a military transport vehicle, one that had an upper deck large enough to hold several heavily armed soldiers.

The picture quality was terrible. And there was no audio to speak of, other than the grind of the truck's engine and some off-color bantering between the men. It was the kind of good-natured ribbing Clay and his friends used to give one another while watching University of Georgia football games.

But how could the soldiers be so carefree? Didn't they know what was about to happen?

Her heart constricted painfully in her chest. How was she going to watch these men die?

She wanted to rail at Wolf for making her sit through this. She glanced over at him, ready to tell him what she thought of his underhanded tactics, but then she noticed the tense look on his face. He didn't want to watch this video any more than she did.

"Why are you putting us through this?" she asked, more than a little angry at him.

"Because you need to see for yourself the sort of danger you're heading into." Determination exuded out of him.

"There are other ways," she whispered.

"If I thought that were true we wouldn't be sitting here now."

Frowning, she returned her gaze to the screen and braced for the inevitable explosion.

The image was bumpier now that the highway had turned into a long stretch of uneven pavement.

One moment the soldiers were driving along, with an endless expanse of desert flanking each side of the road, the next moment...

Boom!

The camera jerked.

And then the image blurred, fading to black.

Unfortunately, the audio still worked. "Get out, get out, get out," someone yelled.

The soldiers were still alive. "Thank God," Hailey murmured.

But before she could discover their ultimate fate, Wolf reached over and clicked the Enter key again.

The image disappeared. Only to be replaced by another.

This one was from the same camera angle, but the truck moved at a snail's pace along a city street amid heavy civilian traffic.

"That's Baghdad," Wolf told her.

Hailey ignored him, her gaze riveted to the screen. Hot tears of frustration filled her eyes. Why couldn't she look away?

She didn't have long to ponder before another...

Boom!

This time, the explosion came from several yards up

ahead of the military vehicle. The sound of screeching tires was all Hailey caught before Wolf clicked a button and another video began.

She sat through three more explosions before she slammed the laptop shut and glared at Wolf. "Enough."

Conviction flickered over his harsh features, but Hailey also saw the haunted look below the hard emotion. The videos had disturbed him as much as they had her.

She opened her mouth to speak, but he cut her off. "*Now* do you see how dangerous it is over there?"

The grief in him was palpable. Clearly, this hideous little exercise had backfired on him. And now he was the one most disturbed by the explosions, both guilt-ridden and filled with regret. The poor man needed redemption. What he didn't understand was the Lord had already given it to him. He just hadn't accepted it yet.

The instinct to push him down the path toward healing made Hailey speak too quickly, with little finesse. "All you managed to prove was how random the violence is over there. *In fact,* the only similarity I saw in those five videos was the haphazard nature of the explosions."

A muscle shifted in his jaw. "That wasn't my point."

Oh, she knew what his point had been. "Regardless. That's what I'm taking away from this. And so should you. The death of your men was not your fault, Wolf. Please, hear me." She pinned him with her stare. "It wasn't your fault."

For a tense moment he just sat there, blinking at her with a glazed look in his eyes. Then he lowered his head and a shiver ran through him. It didn't take all three of

Hailey's college degrees to figure out Wolf was back in the desert, grappling with painful memories.

"This isn't about me." His head snapped up and he looked fully aware of his surroundings. Too aware. "Why won't you accept how dangerous the region is?" He all but growled the question at her.

"I'm not an imbecile. I *know* it's dangerous over there. But I won't cower my way through life. Not anymore." She stood, slapped her palms on the table and glared down at him. "If I die over there, then I die. But at least I'll know I gave my life serving the Lord."

"No." Making a sound of anguish deep in his throat, Wolf rose from the table and yanked her into his arms. "You can't die. Not on my watch."

Hearing the fear in his voice, she pressed her cheek against his chest and sighed. "Oh, Wolf, don't you see? If I stay here, I'll die a slow death of the soul, from a life of superficiality and meaninglessness. Short-term trips to places like Jamaica and Haiti aren't enough. I have to make a bigger commitment."

"I don't buy that." He shoved away from her. The rush of hostility on his face chilled her to the marrow. "There is nothing in the Bible that says you have to climb on an airplane to serve the Lord. You can serve right here, in Savannah. I know of several soup kitchens and at least one homeless shelter that could use your help tomorrow, if not sooner."

Technically he was correct. But in Hailey's case "climbing on an airplane" was the only way for her to achieve her goal, the only way to honor Clay's sacrifice.

She had to make him understand. "Wolf, please, let's sit back down and start this conversation over."

His expression darkened. "We've both said enough for one night."

He spun away from her and left the kitchen without another word.

Oh, no. He wasn't getting off that easily.

"Don't run away from me," she said. "We had too good of a time today to end on this harsh note."

He stopped, unmoving, practically frozen in midstep. "You're right. We did have a good day together." He heaved a sigh. "But I need time to think about everything you've said. Give me that, Hailey."

She reached up to touch his back, but stopped short, her fingers hovering just shy of making a connection.

"Okay, I'll leave you alone." *For now,* she added silently to herself.

Keeping his gaze averted, he shrugged into his jacket. "I'll call you tomorrow."

In the next heartbeat, he was gone.

Chapter Eleven

He didn't call.

Not the next day, like he'd said. Or the next. Or even the next. Nearly an entire week passed without a word from Wolf. Hailey tried not to take his silence personally. After all, she'd given him a lot to think about. Nevertheless, she couldn't help wondering…

Why hadn't he called?

She felt her eyes go a little weepy as she watched him conduct the second half of their weekly survival class. He hadn't looked at her once in the last thirty minutes. In fact, he hadn't looked at her at all since she'd arrived. Coupled with his authoritative tone and systematic manner he'd adopted for tonight's lesson, Wolf might as well be a complete stranger to her.

More than a little irritated, Hailey abandoned all pretense of paying attention to his detailed explanation on how to build a fire and moved to the back of the classroom. She felt better, more in control, now that she was standing rather than sitting.

Perched against the wall, she followed Wolf with her gaze. Her heart tripped at the sight of him moving casually through the room as he spoke. He was almost feline in his movement, like a big jungle cat on the hunt. As if to add to the untamed picture, he wore all black tonight—black jeans, black shirt, black leather jacket.

Talk about fighting dirty.

Why did the man have to be that attractive, and that appealing, when all Hailey wanted to do was ignore him?

She deserved to be angry at him. She had that right. Or so she told herself. But all she really felt was sad. And maybe a little lonely.

She'd opened her heart to Wolf, and she'd thought he'd opened his as well, at least a little. He wouldn't have shared the story of his painful childhood if he didn't have feelings for her. She knew him well enough to know he was too private of a person to open his soul to just anyone.

But she wasn't sure their relationship would ever progress beyond an awkward friendship.

Not with his promise to Clay standing between them.

"You're scowling."

Hailey jerked at the sound of the softly spoken words, barely audible but discernible all the same. She hadn't heard J.T. join her. Then again, he was another one who moved with catlike grace, despite his disability.

Sighing over the interruption, she rolled her gaze in his direction. "I'm not scowling. I'm just paying very close attention to the lesson."

J.T. didn't look convinced. "Okay."

"I am."

"Sure. Sure." He had the audacity to smirk. "Whatever you say, Hailey."

"J.T. I—" She slammed her mouth shut. This was ridiculous, carrying on an argument in hushed tones.

Especially when Hailey had far more important matters on her mind, like how to break through the invisible wall Wolf had erected between them.

She wanted to be left alone to think. Although...

Given his history, maybe J.T. could shed some light on Wolf's recent change in behavior.

She motioned him to follow her into the hallway.

Once they were out of earshot of the class, J.T. broke the silence first. "What's wrong, Hailey?"

His question took her by surprise. "Who said anything was wrong?"

"I know you well enough to know when something's bothering you." He gave her one of his shrewd pastor looks. "Or maybe I should say...*someone*."

By the practical no-nonsense tone of his voice, it was clear J.T. was firmly entrenched in the role of pastor. Under the circumstances, that worked for Hailey. "You're right. I am upset."

"Is it Wolf?"

She answered truthfully. "Yes."

"What has he done?"

"He's done nothing. *Nothing* at all." And wasn't that the real problem here?

That Wolf was allowing his promise to Clay to overshadow everything else between them, to the point of completely shutting Hailey out now that they'd come to yet another impasse?

Although Hailey admired Wolf's commitment to her brother, she sensed his guilt was the driving force behind his actions as much as his inner sense of integrity.

J.T. shifted next to her, the movement drawing her eyes to his injured leg. A silent reminder of his own tragic past. "You and Wolf have been hanging out, right?"

"A little." He shoved his hands into his pockets. "We've had a few lunches together, discussed the survival classes, stuff like that."

Oh, they'd talked about more, Hailey sensed it by J.T.'s professional manner. He was in pastor-mode and wasn't going to reveal anything else on the matter.

We'll see about that.

"How much do you know about Wolf's days in Iraq?" she asked.

"Enough to know I've been where he is now." He didn't have to elaborate. Although Hailey wasn't privy to the particulars of J.T.'s time in the military, she knew he'd been blown up with his men. Just like Wolf.

Hailey knew she could dance around what she most wanted to discuss with him, or she could be direct. Since she had never been one to avoid the tough issues she pressed on. "Wolf blames himself for his men's deaths."

As soon as she blurted out the words, she realized his guilt was really the crux of the matter. If Wolf could accept the fact that he was the victim of a random act of violence rather than the cause, he would begin the healing process.

But how to get him there? Maybe J.T. had some ideas.

"By missing the signs of the IED he thinks he caused the accident," she added when she realized J.T. hadn't responded to her earlier remark.

Still maintaining his silence, he gave her a noncommittal nod, neither confirming nor denying whether this information was news to him.

"On the other hand," she continued, holding his gaze, "I don't blame him for Clay's death."

"That's good." Yet again, the pastor tone and distant manner revealed nothing of J.T.'s thoughts.

In her blazing frustration, Hailey wanted to shake the man for his lack of cooperation. She resisted. Barely. "How can I make him see the truth?"

"You can't."

That was not the answer she was looking for. "But surely there's something I can do."

J.T. shook his head. "I'm sorry, Hailey. You can give him your patience and understanding, but the rest is up to Wolf."

She slammed her fisted hands against her sides. "I hate feeling this helpless."

"Waiting is hard for all of us, but this is between Wolf and the Lord. Trust that God is already at work in him. He'll bring your soldier to healing. In His time, not yours."

As much as Hailey wanted to argue the point, she knew he was right. Like it or not, she had to wait on the Lord.

"Thanks, J.T. That's not really what I wanted to hear, but I can't deny the logic in your words."

"Not just logic, Hailey. Truth."

"Of course."

"Now that we've settled that." He offered his arm in a gallant gesture still common in the South. "Let's get you back to class so you can learn how to light a fire."

Sage words if ever she'd heard them.

Wolf noticed the exact moment Hailey and J.T. returned to the classroom. Both looked lost in their own thoughts. Whatever they'd discussed in the hallway must have been heavy stuff.

He expected Hailey to look up any minute and scowl

at him, like she'd done all evening. But she quietly returned to her place against the wall and proceeded to stare at her feet.

He'd never seen her that subdued. He started to go to her, to find out what was wrong, see if he could help, but then he realized he was in the middle of teaching a class.

Fortunately, he'd covered enough for one night.

"And that's how to build a fire under the best and worst conditions." He shifted his weight back on one foot then shot a quick glance over the assembled group. "Any remarks, questions, complaints, concerns?"

Several hands shot into the air.

He smiled at the obvious enthusiasm in the room. After only two lessons, Wolf was growing to respect these people and their commitment.

They weren't misguided do-gooders with more heart than sense, like he'd first thought. They truly wanted to serve their God, for all the right reasons, and with a fiery passion that humbled him.

Their dedication made Wolf long to have his own calling. But why would the Lord use a man like him, when there were so many out there who hadn't made his colossal mistakes?

Unhappy with the direction of his thoughts, Wolf forced his mind back on task and began fielding questions.

As he spoke, his gaze shifted in Hailey's direction.

She hadn't moved from her spot on the wall, and she was still staring at her feet. She must really be upset with him. Who could blame her? He'd told her he would call and he hadn't.

Not because he'd been avoiding the hard conversation, but because he hadn't known where to *start* the conversation.

Now he regretted his indecision. He didn't like hurting Hailey. It left an empty feeling inside him.

Holding his smile in place, he focused on answering the next question about waterproof matches. "Yes," he replied. "Carrying a small box with you at all times would be wise. As to where to purchase them, any sporting goods or local hardware store should have a variety of choices. But if cost is a factor, you can make your own."

"Really?" someone asked. "How?"

Wolf glanced at the clock mounted over the doorway. He'd promised J.T. he'd have everyone out of here by 2100. It was 2102. "You'll have to wait until next week for that answer. I'll bring written instructions for everyone to take home with them."

Enthusiastic murmurs filled the room. They were actually excited about making their own matches.

This time Wolf's smile felt real as he ran his gaze over the group. "Anything else?"

No one raised their hand. Just as well. He was all talked out. "Okay, then. We're done for the night." He gathered his materials and stuffed them quickly into his bag. "Everyone have a good week."

He stepped to his left so J.T. could join him and say the final prayer of the night. But the pastor didn't move from the back of the room. Instead, he caught Wolf's gaze and said, "Why don't you close us in prayer, Captain Wolfson."

Say what?

The muscles in Wolf's back immediately stiffened. J.T. wanted him to pray? Out loud? In front of all these people? Sweat broke out on his brow.

Was the man kidding?

Apparently not. J.T. hadn't moved off the back wall. Not one inch.

Torn between bolting and getting the job done, Wolf stood frozen in place, on the verge of panic like he'd never experienced before.

He'd faced enemy fire less terrifying than this room of eager, wide-eyed idealists waiting for him to pray for them.

He slowly bowed his head, but not before he looked desperately in Hailey's direction. She wasn't looking down anymore. And she wasn't scowling. She was smiling, *at him,* with a look of genuine encouragement in her gaze.

Feeling stronger, he closed his eyes. "Lord…I…"

He looked up again, feeling hopelessly lost. Hailey mouthed the words: *You can do it.*

He swallowed and started again. His voice stronger this time, he said, "Thank you, Lord, for this time together. I ask that You send us out this week with courage and faith. And may we honor You in everything we do…in Jesus' name. A…*Amen.*"

Low chatter and the rustle of people leaving their seats filled the air. He must have done an okay job with the prayer, even if his words had been a bit generic. At least no one had laughed, or snorted in disgust.

Needing something—*anything*—to make him feel less exposed, Wolf looked at Hailey again. She smiled at him. With the same sweet look in her eyes as before. He couldn't understand why she wasn't holding a grudge against him for not calling her.

She baffled him. But right now, as he stared at all that acceptance in her eyes, Wolf couldn't help himself. He smiled back.

That was all the encouragement she needed. She muttered something to J.T., then broke away from him and headed for the front of the room.

Wolf forced himself to remain where he was. Nonchalant. Normal. Nothing out of the ordinary here. Except...

His heartbeat had decided to kick into overdrive. And a trickle of sweat rolled down his back. Hailey O'Brien made him nervous. A completely new and terrifying sensation.

Fortunately, she wasn't the only one who wanted to talk to him. By the time she made it to the front of the room, Wolf was already surrounded by a handful of people asking him rapid-fire questions all at once.

He did his best to answer them, one by one. Patient. Smooth. In control.

Who was he kidding?

He couldn't make his mind work properly. Not with Hailey hovering just outside the circle of people, watching, waiting calmly for her turn to speak to him.

Once Wolf had answered all the questions, he turned his full attention onto Hailey.

Every muscle in his body tensed. There was something different about her tonight, a curious blend of patience and consideration.

"Hi," she said, her eyes revealing nothing.

"Hi," he said back, feeling like an awkward teenager in the throes of his first crush. The woman fascinated him in ways he hadn't begun to untangle in his mind.

He had a thousand things he wanted to say to her, now that they were face-to-face. But just like every time he'd picked up the phone this week to call her, he was stuck without an opening line.

First and foremost, he needed to apologize for not

calling her. Except…how did he do that? What could he say that wouldn't come off sounding trite?

"So, here's the thing," she began, her eyes still unreadable. "We ended things on a pretty dramatic note last time we saw one another."

"You could say that." He swallowed, determined to get his apology out before she continued with whatever else she had to say. "Look, Hailey, I'm sorry I—"

"Don't mention it." She waved a hand in disregard, cutting off his apology midsentence. "You've been busy. The important thing is that we're both here now, feeling unnecessarily awkward with one another. Let's not do this. Let's just move on, okay?"

Stunned she was going to let him off that easily, he cleared his throat. "I like that idea."

He wanted to say more but out of the corner of his eye he saw J.T. bearing down on them. Whatever the pastor had to say, Wolf didn't want to hear it right now.

"Let's get out of here," he suggested, keeping his eyes on J.T.

Following his gaze, Hailey made a soft sound of impatience in her throat. "We agree on something at last."

Even though Wolf gave J.T. a back-off glare the pastor closed the distance with clipped strides. "Just wanted to thank you for another great class, Captain." He held up his fist, knuckles facing Wolf.

Wolf forced down his impatience and pounded J.T.'s fist with his own. "Thanks."

Lowering his hand, J.T. looked from Wolf to Hailey then back again. He repeated the process two more times, a slow smile tugging at his lips on the last pass.

"What?" Wolf demanded.

"I see I'm interrupting. I'll just leave you two alone so you can speak in private."

With a surprisingly quick gait, he hustled out of the room, practically dragging the last two stragglers with him. He shut the door behind them with a decided click.

Okay. Good. Wolf was completely alone with Hailey. Here was his chance. "I really am sorry I didn't call you all week."

She regarded him with a complicated array of female emotions no man could ever hope to decipher. "Understandable. I gave you a lot to think about."

"Nevertheless," he said carefully, not sure why she was being so nice about this. "My silence was rude."

"Okay, yes, it *was* rude. But you're forgiven." Her tone held nothing but sincerity. The woman was actually letting him off the hook. No questions asked. No explanations needed.

Grace personified.

Wolf's heart dipped in his chest. But then reality set in. "Hailey, I like you," he admitted. "More than I can put into words."

"But…?"

Grimacing, he stuffed his hands into his pockets. "Who said there's a 'but'?"

"There's always a 'but' when a man starts a sentence with those three horrible words, *I like you*." She sighed dramatically. "It's the kiss of death to any relationship."

They had a relationship?

Of course they did. But not like she meant. And not like he wanted.

"Okay, you're right. There is a 'but.' You see, no matter how much I like you, and would love to explore what comes next, we can't forget that Clay is standing between us. And probably always will."

Even if Wolf managed to keep Hailey out of the Middle East, even if she didn't grow to hate him because of it, they would never know if they were together because of their shared bond over Clay or because they truly worked as a couple.

Talk about a stalemate.

She notched her chin a fraction higher. "Then we have to get to know one another without him around."

Not possible. "How do you suggest we do that?"

"We go somewhere that doesn't remind either of us of my brother."

He snorted. "That place doesn't exist."

Her gaze turned thoughtful. Planting one hand on her hip, she tapped her chin with the other. "We just need to find a way to understand one another's position better, without your promise to Clay muddying the process."

As if he was the only stubborn one in the room. "Or your determination to honor his death complicating things, either."

"Fair enough."

She fell silent and got a faraway look in her eyes. "Perhaps instead of looking to the future, we have to go back to the past. Yes, that just might be the answer."

He hated that idea. His past was best left buried. He regretted revealing the ugly circumstances of his childhood to this woman, yet it was too late to recall the words. Besides, Wolf wasn't ready to quit on her, on them. "What did you have in mind?"

"I need to introduce you to the person I used to be. Then you'll better understand the person I've become and why I have to go to the Middle East as planned."

Why would Wolf want to meet the old Hailey? He liked the new one just fine.

"Come on, Wolf. We have to try something."

She seemed pretty definite, like she had it all figured out in her head. Which did not instill a lot of confidence in him. On the contrary. "What sort of 'something' are we talking about here?"

"Well…" She secured her gaze on a spot just off center of his face. "I have to attend a dinner and silent auction this weekend. We're raising money for inner-city children."

Despite the noble cause, Wolf felt his shoulders bunch with tension. "Where's this event being held?"

"At the country club."

No way. He'd been to a country club once. In college, with a girl he'd been dating at the time. He couldn't remember the particulars, but he remembered feeling uncomfortable and out of place all night long. The evening had ended badly. "I don't do country clubs."

"But surely you'll make an exception this time." She touched his arm and gave him "the look," the same one that had prompted him to fire up his motorcycle against his better judgment.

The woman had a way of making him forget logic and reason.

He choked down a gulp of air.

"The dinner is the most efficient way for me to show you who I used to be."

He didn't want to know. No good could come of this. "I don't own a tux," he said, cringing at the note of desperation he heard in his voice.

"Wear your dress blues." She gave him a good, long once-over. "It's hard to resist a man in uniform."

Doomed. He was absolutely powerless in the face

of all that female persuasion. "All right. I'll go." He
grasped at the remaining scrap of his pride. "Under one
condition."

Her lips curled into a feline smile. "Name it."

Oh, she was feeling smug now. *Let's see how long
that lasts.*

"I'll brave the country club with you—" he nearly
choked on the words "—if you go skydiving with me
first."

She gave him a burst of strangled laughter. Her gaze
darted around the room, landing everywhere but on him.
"I couldn't possibly jump out of an airplane."

Of course not. Hence the suggestion. "That's my
condition, Hailey." He held firm. "Take it or leave it."

She gaped at him for several seconds. "You're
serious."

"I am." He gave her his best wolf grin. Yeah, he had
a few tricks himself. "Not to worry, though. I'll make
sure you get proper training before you have to jump
out on your own."

"You want me to jump a…alone?" she squeaked. "Not
hooked to someone who knows what he's doing?"

"I'll be right next to you, holding on until you pull
the rip cord."

"I…I…"

"Where's that new adventurous streak of yours?" he
goaded. "The one that's gonna carry you halfway across
the world to a war-torn region?"

She muttered something under her breath, the words
sounding jumbled and not very nice at all. Something
about a baboon and unfair tactics and…

Best not to decode the rest.

"Come on, Hailey. All you have to do is go skydiving

with me—" he held a perfectly timed pause "—and then I'll brave the big, bad country club with you."

He crossed his arms in front of his chest and smiled. He had her. There would be no country club in his future.

But then she straightened her shoulders and pulled her lips into a tight little rosebud of defiance. "All right, big boy. You're on. I'll go skydiving with you."

Yeah, right.

He leaned in close to her ear, turning the screws. "Bring your sunscreen, baby, we're going to get pretty high up there. Wouldn't want you to get burned."

"Don't you worry about me, *baby.* I'll be fine. Super-duper fine." She poked him hard in the chest.

"Just make sure your dress uniform is clean by Saturday night. I want to show you off to all the fine ladies of Savannah. They love getting to know young, good-looking, *single* military officers."

He nearly choked on his own breath.

Somehow, while he'd been congratulating himself on his own brilliance, she'd done it again. The feisty little tiger had turned the tables on him.

Hailey O'Brien was turning out to be one formidable woman.

And Wolf was turning out to be a man who couldn't say no to her.

Chapter Twelve

The sound of the airplane engine reminded Hailey far too much of Stella's obnoxious growl. Perhaps that explained why she couldn't stop shaking. Or maybe she wasn't really shaking at all. It was hard to tell with the two-seater airplane vibrating like an overexcited Chihuahua.

Wolf's muscle car had nothing on this contraption.

When they'd arrived at the airfield with the jumpmaster, the exterior of the tiny airplane had looked passable enough. But then all three of them had taken their places inside and Hailey had discovered the interior, save the pilot's seat, had been gutted so that it could hold extra skydivers.

Now that they'd taken off, she glanced over the jumpmaster's head at the gaping hole on their right, the spot where a door was supposed to be.

Gulping for air, she quickly turned her head the other way. But her gaze landed on the grinning man beside her and her stomach dipped to her toes.

Wolf's expression held far too much glee. And maybe even a little bit of crazy.

Why wasn't he more concerned they were about to

jump out of an airplane at thirteen thousand feet? That was over two miles above the ground.

And they were in a flying tin can, with only a few scraps of material, strapped to their backs, preventing them from falling, literally, straight to their deaths.

Hailey wasn't just scared. She was petrified.

Wolf must have read her mind, because he reached out and squeezed her hand. "Don't worry," he yelled over the airplane's roar. "I packed our chutes myself."

That gave her a measure of relief. Unfortunately, it wasn't enough.

She slammed her eyes shut, telling herself this was a large, courageous step in the right direction to becoming a woman of adventure. If she lived through this, Wolf had to go to the country club with her tonight. The two didn't seem equally scary in her mind, but apparently they were in Wolf's. It was all about perception, she supposed.

Keeping her eyes firmly shut, she ran through the instructions the jumpmaster, Ken, had drilled into her head all morning. As soon as the pilot cut the engine— and wasn't that a frightening prospect?—the three of them were supposed to climb on the wing of the airplane and fall backward so they could clear the airplane.

She was then supposed to assume a position similar to a belly flop and simply enjoy the ride for seven thousand feet. Wolf and Ken would be on either side, guiding her. When the time came, they would release her and she would pull the rip cord on her own.

This, of course, was all assuming she was still conscious. A high possibility since the temperature was at least thirty degrees colder at this altitude.

She felt a tap on her shoulder. Unhappy with the interruption, she cracked open one eye.

"Tell me that isn't a spectacular view," Wolf shouted, pointing to the ground below.

Taking a deep breath, Hailey stabbed a glance out the window. They were flying directly above the ocean, but the shoreline was in clear sight.

Okay, yes, the view was beautiful. Unfortunately, Hailey couldn't tell Wolf she agreed with him. She was too busy remembering the jumpmaster's warning about landing in the ocean. If that little disaster occurred and she didn't get out of the parachute quickly enough, the water could drag her under. To death by drowning.

And Wolf considered this fun?

The man had a death wish. Pure and simple.

Jamaica, Haiti, the Middle East, whether she spent a week or a lifetime in any of those locales, she didn't think she'd feel as concerned about her life as she did now.

The pilot cut the engine.

The sudden silence took Hailey by surprise and she nearly choked on her own gasp.

"It's go time," Wolf said cheerfully.

Lord, please, please, get me through this alive. I don't want to go splat on the ground.

"I'm ready."

She quit thinking so hard and let her training kick in. Just as Ken had instructed, she followed him onto the wing of the airplane, one terrifying step at a time.

Clinging to the metal structure, she scooted over far enough for Wolf to join them.

She didn't dare look down.

Wolf's hand closed over hers. "I'm right here with you. Every step of the way."

She gave him a shaky smile.

"We do this together," Ken reminded her.

"Right. Together." She turned her palm and pressed it flat against Wolf's. Her fear cut in half.

"On three." He squeezed her hand then let go. "One. Two."

"Three," she shouted and then leaned backward.

Her feet tumbled over her head.

She only had time for impressions after that. Wolf and Ken were still on either side of her, holding her steady. The wind slapped her in the face so hard she could barely breathe, the noise of it screaming through her ears at a deafening level.

She checked the altimeter on her wrist, shocked to see she'd already fallen three thousand feet.

Wolf tugged on her jumpsuit. She glanced in his direction. He gave her a thumbs-up.

A few more seconds passed before Wolf and Ken let her go. That was her signal to take control. She threw the rip cord and felt rather than heard the Velcro release her parachute.

She braced for a hard jerk as the parachute began filling with air, but her feet floated gently below her.

Amazed at how easy the transition had been from free fall to floating, Hailey reached for the toggles. She practiced steering by pulling on one and then the other. At last, she allowed herself to look down.

The view was amazing. Blue sky, green water, sandy beach. How could anybody witness all this beauty and not believe in God?

With her senses poised on high alert, Hailey drank in the experience. Every sight, sound and smell consumed her.

Both Wolf and Ken landed several minutes ahead of her. Wolf gathered his parachute with quick, jerky tugs, all the while searching the sky for her.

She waved at him.

He waved back and then dropped the chute so that he could make a cradle with his arms, as if he were waiting to catch her if she fell.

It was a joke, but a really sweet one with all kinds of symbolism she didn't have time to unravel.

Landing on the beach turned out to be somewhat anticlimcatic. She pulled hard on the toggles and hit the ground, feetfirst, with a soft thud.

Joy burst through her.

"I did it. I did it. I did it." Hopping from one foot to the other, she pumped her fists in the air in her own version of a happy-dance.

Wolf scooped her up into a hug that lifted her several feet in the air.

Overwhelmed with emotion, she clung to him, wrapping her arms around his neck. "That was amazing."

He set her on the ground and kissed her smack on the lips. "*You're* amazing."

They stared at each other. Both breathing hard. She wanted this man in her life. Always. But did he want to be in hers? Or was his promise to Clay the only thing keeping him here?

She hated that she didn't know the answer to that, that he might not know for sure, either.

Wolf broke eye contact first and went about systematically removing the rest of his parachute, mainly the now-empty container still strapped to his back.

Ken joined them and gave Hailey a high five. "Well done, beautiful. One of the best first jumps I've ever witnessed."

"It was fantastic."

He helped her out of her parachute then turned to Wolf. "I need to get back to post. I have a buddy picking me up at the lighthouse. You two need a ride into town?"

Wolf shook his head. "We dropped off my car earlier this morning."

"Good enough." He smiled at Hailey and then handed her a small business card. "Let me know if you ever want to do this again. I'm only a phone call away."

She thought she heard Wolf growl. Surely she was mistaken? "Thanks, Ken," she said. "But once was enough for me."

"If you change your mind…"

She smiled. "I'll call."

"Sounds good." He walked over to Wolf, said something in a low tone. Wolf nodded. They both laughed, then Ken slapped him on the back.

"All right. See you two later." Ken headed out, waving a hand over his head in farewell.

Watching him leave with his parachute bunched in his arms, Hailey realized she was still jumping from foot to foot. "I can't seem to stand still."

"It's the adrenaline." Wolf slanted an unreadable glance in her direction. "It'll wear off soon."

She wanted it to wear off now. She hated this nagging, uncomfortable feeling, as if she were ready to jump out of her own skin. Too many emotions collided into one another. Excitement, fear, relief, joy and something else, something darker, something she couldn't quite name.

"So." She bounced toward Wolf. "What happens when the adrenaline finally wears off?"

He didn't like the question. She could see it in the way his hands paused over folding his parachute.

"You're gonna feel exhausted in a few minutes. Maybe even a little depressed. But it'll go away soon enough and then you'll be ready for your next jolt. *Jump.* I meant, jump."

No, he'd meant jolt. "That sounds almost like…like… an addiction."

He didn't respond. But the uneasy look in his eyes told her she was right.

Was Wolf hooked on adrenaline? Was that why he drove a ridiculously fast car, owned a motorcycle, jumped out of airplanes?

"Wolf? Is that why you do this?" She waved her hand in a wide arc. "For the rush?"

"No." He answered quickly, seeming very sure of himself.

"Then why?"

"It's complicated."

She waited for him to say more. But he just stared at the water. And stared. And stared.

Why wouldn't he explain himself?

Still looking out over the ocean, he discarded his parachute and then sat down, right there where he'd been standing. He drew his legs up and caged his knees inside his clasped hands.

Hailey joined him on the sand, hugging her own legs to her chest.

"I don't know why I jump out of airplanes, Hailey. I don't analyze it. I just do it."

There was more to it than that, but for now she accepted his explanation, determined not to push him. She sensed his reasons were tied to what happened to him in Iraq, but she wasn't sure. The not-knowing was the hard part.

For several minutes they sat in silence. Hailey watched the waves crash onto the shore, one on top of another, never ending, never ceasing. Like God's grace, freely offered to all who wanted it.

"If I was going to analyze my motives," Wolf said at last, "I'd probably say it's a test."

"A test?" she repeated. "For who? You?"

"No." He drew a circle in the sand with the toe of his boot. "I guess I'm testing God. I need to know if I was really meant to survive that attack, or if the Lord made a mistake. I need to know if *I* was a mistake."

Tears filled her eyes. How could such a courageous, competent man think he was a mistake, when he had so much to offer the world? "Oh, Wolf. God doesn't sit on some royal throne up in heaven, picking and choosing who lives and who dies."

He lowered his chin to his chest. "What if He does?"

She gathered her words carefully. "I don't know why the others died. Some things we'll never completely understand until we get to heaven. It was just their time. You were left behind for a reason. The Heavenly Father has a plan for your life."

"He can't use me." A devastated look flashed in his eyes. "I can't be trusted. Look what happened on that roadside."

Lord, he's not hearing me. "You can't keep blaming yourself, Wolf. It's unproductive."

He buried his face in his hands. His words were muffled, but she thought she heard him say he should have seen the bomb.

"Okay, Wolf, let's go with that. Let's say that, yes, you should have seen the bomb. Now what?"

He dropped his hands and leveled a shocked gaze on her. "What do you mean?"

"Supposing the accident was your fault. What then?

Do you spend the rest of your life making amends? Or maybe you chase the next adrenaline high, until you ultimately kill yourself?"

He flattened his lips into a grim line. "I'm careful."

"Nobody's *that* careful."

He grew silent.

Oh, no. He didn't get to shut down on her now. They'd started down this road. They were going all the way. "If you're right, Wolf, and you are to blame for your men's deaths, then, I repeat, what comes next?"

"I…" He blinked, then shook his head slowly, miserably. "I don't know."

"Well, I do." In fact, she knew exactly what came next. "You forgive yourself. That's what. God has already forgiven you." She leaned forward and touched her lips gently to his cheek. "*I've* forgiven you. Now it's your turn, Wolf."

His eyes hardened. "What? You think everything's going to fall into place after I forgive myself? Is that what you're saying?" His voice held a large amount of bitterness, but Hailey also heard an unmistakable twinge of hope underneath. Just enough to make her feel they'd made progress here today.

"Not all at once. But, yes, Wolf. Everything starts to get better *after* you forgive yourself."

Chapter Thirteen

Wolf stood inside the country club, trying not to feel stiff and uncomfortable among the pretty people of Savannah. While he waited for the coat-check girl to return with his and Hailey's claim checks, he pretended not to notice the wary stares thrown his way, or the wide berth most people gave him.

Obviously, this particular country club didn't have a lot of military personnel among its membership. Like that was a big shocker.

He hid a yawn behind a slow, deep breath. His leg had started to ache hours ago, the lingering pain a constant reminder of what had happened that day in Iraq. Twice now Hailey had sent him reeling with her words of encouragement and forgiveness. She really didn't blame Wolf for her brother's death. He accepted that now, felt blessed by it.

If he was honest with himself, he'd rather be somewhere alone with Hailey, where they could talk, just the two of them. She'd be leaving for Haiti soon and he didn't want her boarding the airplane until matters were a little less volatile between them. Nevertheless, she'd been incredibly brave this morning. It was only fair he held up his end of the bargain tonight.

Compelled, he glanced over at his lovely date. She was still speaking to the elderly couple she'd introduced him to when they'd first arrived. The Pattersons seemed nice enough. He shot a smile in their direction and tried to keep his thoughts clear, but they kept circling back to the conversation he'd had with Hailey on the beach.

Now that she'd forgiven him, she wanted him to forgive himself, as if it were just a matter of changing his mind-set.

Well, forgiveness wasn't something Wolf had much experience with, not with the sort of childhood he'd endured. Survival, now *that* he understood. Wolf had lived the first fifteen years of his life in a vicious cycle of abuse and poverty. But he'd gotten out. Was it now his turn to give back?

A warm sense of destiny settled over him.

In the next moment the coat-check girl returned. He took the two slips she offered him with a smile and then turned back to his date.

His breath hitched in his chest. Hailey stood alone now, under a beacon of golden light, her smile solely for him.

He took a moment to simply enjoy the view.

The woman was all female curves in a fitted green dress. The color matched her glorious eyes. She'd piled her hair on top of her head in a messy array of curls that managed to look very elegant. At first glance her hair looked dark, almost black, but under the light Wolf could see the deep red undertones. The color reminded him of cherry cola. His new favorite drink.

"What?" Hailey cocked her head at him, her brow furrowed into a cute little frown.

He closed the distance a bit more, inhaling her perfume. He loved that spicy, floral scent that was solely hers. "I didn't say anything."

Her frown deepened. "You didn't have to. You have a strange look on your face."

He twirled one of her dark curls between his thumb and forefinger. "I was just admiring the view." He dropped his hand. "If I haven't told you already, you look beautiful tonight, Hailey. Really stunning."

And Wolf was feeling incredibly tender toward her. The sensation made his heart pound so hard his chest hurt. Which wasn't altogether a terrible sensation, just... unsettling.

"Well, I—" She visibly swallowed. "Thank you, Wolf. You look beautiful, too. I mean—" she gave a little self-conscious laugh "—you look handsome. The uniform is working for you."

He leaned in closer, catching another whiff of her precious scent. "But is it working for you?"

"Oh, yeah." Her eyes looked a little dazed. "It's really working for me."

"Then I'm glad I wore it."

They smiled at one another.

"So where do we go next?" he asked, prepared to brave the rest of the evening for Hailey's sake.

"The first room on our left." She hooked her arm through his and tugged him down yet another over-decorated hallway.

"What's in there?"

"The silent auction. Since we have over an hour before the dinner is served I figure we can see if there's anything worth bidding on tonight."

"Sure, why not?"

For the next ten minutes, they meandered through

the room reserved for the silent auction. There were at least a hundred items up for sale.

There were fancy hotel stays with opening bids more than Wolf made in a month. There were weekend getaways, spa treatments, the latest electronic gadgets, lunches with dignitaries. But the one item that really grabbed Wolf's attention was the ridiculous opportunity to spend the afternoon with Uga, the famous bulldog mascot for the University of Georgia.

"Why would anyone want to pay money to spend the day with a glorified mutt," he wondered out loud, looking down the rather long line of handwritten bids. He zeroed in on the most recent number recorded. "Would you look at that, someone bid eight hundred dollars. That's insane."

"Shh." Hailey looked over her shoulder with a horrified expression on her face. "Somebody might hear you."

"Did you just shush me?" he asked, trying not to laugh. "Over a dog named U-G-A?"

She swung back around to glare at him. "Don't you dare make fun of my favorite bulldog." She actually sounded offended. "And, for your information, his name is pronounced *Ugh-ah*."

Apparently, it was up to Wolf to give the woman a reality check. All that oxygen-deprived air in the plane must have left her a little loopy. "He's a dog, Hailey."

"You might want to take note, Captain Wolfson. People around here take their college football very seriously. *And* their mascots."

"Let me guess," he said, trying to keep a straight face. "You went to the University of Georgia and now have an unhealthy fondness for smushed-faced dogs."

"Smushed-faced dogs?" Head high, she yanked a

pen out of her purse. Keeping her eyes glued to his, she scribbled down a bid.

He leaned over and read the outrageous amount. "And you think I'm crazy for jumping out of airplanes?"

"It's for a good cause."

He said nothing, mainly because he liked her all worked up like this. Not that he'd tell her so. He wanted to get out of here in one piece.

Giving in to a smile, Wolf took in the room with a quick swoop. "So this is how you used to raise money for all your causes? Pawning off stuff to the rich folks of Savannah?"

She didn't answer right away, but instead looked around the room as he had done, perhaps trying to see the situation from his perspective. "A silent auction might seem like an odd way to raise money." She lowered her voice. "But some people will only give to a charity if they're getting something in return."

Yeah, he'd already figured that one out on his own. "What percentage of the night's take goes to the kids?"

She blew a tendril of hair away from her face. "All the items are donated, Wolf. The foundation gets a hundred percent of the proceeds."

Well, that was something at least.

"Don't look so disappointed," she said. "This isn't a Christian organization, but the people in attendance do care about their community."

She linked her arm through his and steered him out of the room before he could respond. "Come on, let's go take a look at the gardens. They're beautiful this time of year."

He chuckled at her transparent attempt to change the subject. "Smooth, Hailey. Very smooth."

"The money from the auction is only a portion of what we'll raise tonight," she said, once they left the room.

"How else will you get funding?"

She slid a glance at him from beneath her lowered lashes. "We place a stack of envelopes at every table."

"Envelopes?" He had no idea what that meant. "For what?"

"After the presentation the chairman of the board will get up and ask everyone to consider giving a donation directly to the foundation."

Wolf rubbed a finger over his temple, trying to relinquish the pressure of the headache building behind his eyes. The people were here, like Hailey said, and they were providing money for a good cause, yet something about the evening felt off. He couldn't figure out what.

"Wolf. No matter why the checks are written, the important point is the children win out in the end."

Okay, she had a point. A valid one. "Speaking of which, where are the kids?"

She stopped walking and stared at him. "What do you mean?"

"I haven't seen a single kid here tonight. Why not?" When he was young he would have given anything for the kind of meal they were going to serve later.

"The children can't be here tonight. It wouldn't be... it wouldn't be..." She looked at him helplessly. "Well, it wouldn't be appropriate."

"Why not?"

She gave him a shrug. But something in the gesture increased the tension in him. "Oh, I get it. They aren't good enough for this crowd." Just like he hadn't been good enough when he'd been a kid.

"No." Her hand practically clawed at his arm. "That's

not what I meant at all. This entire evening is about the children, and the rec center we're going to build for them with the money we raise."

"Have you met any of the kids yourself?"

"Well, no." She dropped her head. "But I—"

He didn't wait for the rest. So this was the old Hailey. No wonder she'd been so determined to change. But had she really? She hadn't even met the kids she was supposed to be helping. He picked up his pace, not wanting to continue this discussion.

Hailey followed hard on his heels. She grabbed his arm and dragged him toward a door leading to an outdoor balcony.

The cold slapped him in the face, but she kept dragging him across the marble stones. Click, click, click, her heels struck like hammers to nails.

She stopped abruptly. The night closed in around them, like a phantom. The club's outdoor lighting provided just enough light for Wolf to see Hailey's troubled expression.

"Wolf, try to understand. This isn't a Christian organization."

"You said that already."

She started to say more but then shivered from the cold.

He unbuttoned his coat and wrapped it around her shoulders. They stared at one another for a long, tense moment. She looked so tiny inside his jacket. Lost.

But was he looking at the old Hailey, or the new one? He hated that he didn't know for sure.

Ever since he'd walked into this place he hadn't been able to stop thinking about the life he'd lived as a child, how instead of writing checks for good causes his father had been too busy looking for his next drink. Wolf, like many inner-city kids, had alternated between scrapping for food and dodging his father's fist.

"After tonight," he said, "the people here will go back to their cozy existence where the most important problem they have to face is the thread count in their bedsheets."

He knew he sounded bitter, but he couldn't untangle the ball of tension in his gut. "They don't understand the despair that comes from wondering if there's going to be a meal tomorrow."

Not like Wolf understood it. Terrible memories bombarded him. Once, when his dad had gone on a month-long bender, Wolf had survived solely on the free lunches he'd gotten at school. The weekends had been nightmarish, but he'd lived through them.

In the end, the Army had been his ticket out.

But not every kid could take that route.

Something has to be done for the rest. The thought was so clear in his head he wondered where it had come from.

"Oh, Wolf." Hailey shifted closer to him. "This is what I've been trying to tell you ever since we met."

"Come again?"

"Don't get me wrong, these types of functions serve a purpose. But you're right. Many of the people in there are just like you described. And for the last twenty-five years of my life, I was one of them."

He heard the familiar sorrow in her voice, but tonight it sounded more like guilt than regret.

"I never got my hands dirty, Wolf, because no one ever taught me how."

"That's your excuse?"

"No. Not an excuse. An explanation of who I used to be. But everything changed for me when Clay died.

He'd been planting seeds for months prior to the day of the bombing. His death gave me the final push."

Wolf admired the courage it must have taken Hailey to take that hard look at her life. But her role model had been a hardened soldier stuck in a war zone. If only Wolf could see what Clay had put in his e-mails he might have a better idea how to proceed.

"I don't want to be insulated anymore." Hailey wrapped his coat tighter around her shoulders. "I want to get to know the people I serve, personally. I want to live with them, cry with them, find joy and hope with them. I did a little of that in Jamaica. It's what I hope to do in Haiti and ultimately in the Middle East."

Admirable, yes, but again Wolf was struck with the notion that Hailey was still living with blinders on, unable to see the need right next to her. "You don't have to go to the Middle East to do what you just described."

"It's where Clay went."

Yep, now he knew for certain. Her perspective was skewed. "Your brother was sent to the Middle East. Stop romanticizing what he did over there. He was a soldier who lived in a war zone, and all that that implies. People are killed on a daily basis. Some are even tortured in brutal, unimaginable ways."

"Exactly." Her conviction all but radiated out of her. "There are innocent people who live in those war zones. People who aren't trained soldiers. Somebody has to care about them. Somebody has to show them the love of Christ. And that somebody is going to be me."

"How do you know it's supposed to be you?"

"I just do."

"That's not good enough. I want to hear specifics."

She fell silent, and then sank onto a wrought-iron bench.

Wolf sat down next to her and took her hand gently in his. "Don't you think I've been paying attention at our survival classes?"

She slid a glance in his direction. "What's that supposed to mean?"

"Your friends have taught me as much as I've taught them, maybe more. A person doesn't go on a mission trip to prove a point. She goes because she's called."

"I was called." She snatched her hand free. "To the Middle East."

Maybe she had been. Maybe. "Tell me the moment you knew for sure."

She climbed hastily to her feet, spun around and then clutched at the railing behind her. "When Clay died."

As though a light turned on in his head, Wolf knew exactly what he had to do next. He had to introduce Hailey to local people in need right here in Savannah.

If, after that, Hailey still believed she'd been called to the Middle East, then Wolf wouldn't stand in her way.

Not that he'd let her go over there unprepared. He'd do what he could to protect her, even if it required him climbing on that airplane with her. It would mean a complete change in his own lifestyle, but if that's what it took to keep her safe, then he'd do it.

Of course, there were a lot of "ifs" that still needed to be settled before life-altering decisions had to be made.

Wolf rose and joined her at the railing, stunned that he was actually thinking about giving up. No, not giving up, getting more information for them both. "What are you doing Wednesday morning?"

"Nothing that can't be rescheduled." Her brows lifted in inquiry. "Why?"

"I want to take you somewhere that might benefit us both."

"Don't you have to work?"

"Not on Wednesday." He'd already scheduled the day off in the hopes of finishing his move into the town house. Now he had a different plan in mind. "I'll pick you up at 0900."

"Where are you planning to take me?"

"Someplace where you can get your hands dirty."

Chapter Fourteen

Wolf found J.T. sitting alone in his office. The pastor was bent over a stack of papers, completely absorbed in his work.

Leaning against the doorjamb, Wolf waited a few beats then broke the silence. "Want to grab some lunch?"

J.T. didn't bother looking up. "I was wondering how long you were going to stand there staring at me."

"You knew I was here?"

Head still bent, J.T. flashed a quick smile. "You're not exactly light on your feet, soldier."

Wolf chuckled. "I'll file that information away for later."

J.T. joined in the laughter. After a moment, he tossed his pen aside and leaned back in his chair, his smile still holding. "Have a seat and tell me what's on your mind."

Wolf hesitated. He hadn't planned to have this conversation here, in the church, but J.T. must have countless resources a mouse click away in his computer. It made sense to take his friend up on his offer. Except...

J.T. might misunderstand this visit, thinking Wolf had

come for guidance rather than a simple list of homeless shelters and soup kitchens.

Feeling mildly uncomfortable, Wolf lowered himself into one of the two chairs facing J.T.'s desk. His gaze landed on a free-standing marble plaque that looked like a generic paperweight at first glance.

He read aloud the Scripture etched in black calligraphy. "I consider my life worth nothing to me, if only I may finish the race and complete the task the Lord Jesus has given me—the task of testifying the Gospel of God's grace. Acts 20:24."

"The senior pastor gave that to me on my first day here," J.T. explained. "It helps me remember that I'm investing my life in the only thing that matters, in a legacy that will live on after I'm gone."

Wolf remained silent, holding perfectly still, moving only the tip of his finger across the bold lettering.

He reread the Scripture, trying to comprehend the meaning behind J.T.'s bold remark. "Do you mean spreading the Gospel?"

"Roger that." J.T. steepled his fingers under his chin and stared at Wolf with a satisfied light in his eyes. "You've come a long way since the first time we met."

Wolf rubbed his leg absently. He supposed he had, from a certain perspective. There wasn't as much anger in him, nor as much despair. The Dream wasn't coming as often, either. He knew he owed much of his healing to Hailey. In their short acquaintance, she'd softened his hard edges and made him want to be a better man.

That wasn't to say Wolf didn't still feel lost at times. And confused. "I have a long way to go."

"We all do," J.T. agreed.

The certainty in the pastor's voice surprised Wolf. "Even you?"

"Especially me." J.T. stared off into space then gave his head a quick shake. "So, what brought on this sudden offer of lunch? You doing okay, adjusting to life back in the States?"

"I'm getting there."

Now why had he admitted that? Why hadn't he told J.T. to mind his own business? Like he had every other time the guy had probed too far into his mental state.

Fingers still braced under his chin, J.T. eyed Wolf with a look that was filled with concern yet also held deep understanding. "What can I do to help you, Captain?"

Wolf's gaze darted around the room. The use of his rank was a clear sign of respect on J.T.'s part, a reminder that they shared a common bond.

"Wolf?"

He drummed his fingers on the arms of the chair, still not looking directly at J.T. This wasn't the way the conversation was supposed to go. Wolf had come here to get a list of local homeless shelters. Nothing more.

You could have done that over the phone, he told himself. Or e-mail.

But he hadn't. He'd sought out J.T. personally, and not just to get the list. He realized that now. Somewhere along the way Wolf had grown to trust J.T., as both a friend and a pastor.

Man up, Wolf. Tell the guy what's really going on.

"Hailey thinks I need to forgive myself for my men's deaths," he blurted out. "She says the bombing wasn't my fault."

As soon as the words slipped from his mouth, he wanted to take them back. But it was too late. The truth was out there, hanging in the room like a heavy, invisible shroud of gloom.

To his credit, J.T. didn't react. He simply continued

sitting in his chair, cool, calm, completely laid-back.
Oddly enough, the guy's casual posture had Wolf relaxing, too.

"What do you think? Do you agree with her?" J.T.
asked.

"I…" He paused to consider the question and not just
answer off the top of his head. "I want to agree with
her, but I don't know if I can. The guilt." He squeezed
his eyes shut a moment. "Sometimes, it's too much to
bear."

A series of creaks and groans filled the air as J.T.
shifted in his chair. The pastor no longer looked calm,
but very, very intense. "Yet, you're here now. Talking
to me. That's a good thing."

Wolf wasn't so sure.

J.T. leaned closer, just a fraction more, but enough to
make Wolf sit up straighter. "Tell me why you sought
me out today."

Wolf rubbed a hand over his face. "Because I'm tired
of feeling like this. I'm tired of shouldering this burden
alone."

"Good." J.T. nodded. "That's the first step, admitting
the problem."

Wolf should feel pressured. Uncomfortable. He didn't
feel either. Instead, he experienced a strange sense of
peace now that he'd shared his concerns. "What do I do
next?"

J.T. sat back, assuming his casual pose once again.
"I'm afraid there's no magic formula. You're already
serving here at the church. You're making a difference
with a lot of people. That's a start."

J.T.'s words confused him. "I'm just teaching survival
skills."

"Your classes are serving a purpose for the Kingdom. Keep teaching them."

"That's all?" It didn't seem enough.

"No. Serving is just the beginning. You might also want to spend time in prayer, read the Word, seek counsel from other Christians." J.T. leaned forward. "But, Wolf, nothing will help until you give this up to the Lord. Healing starts with surrender."

Surrender. Wolf balked at the concept. It went against everything he knew as a soldier. But maybe J.T. was right. Maybe he had to give this up to God, rather than agonize over details he couldn't control. The problem was, handling details was what he did best.

Look where that's gotten you.

Wolf shuddered at the thought.

"I want you to listen to me, Captain." J.T. captured Wolf's gaze with an unyielding glare. "We live in a fallen world. Life here on earth is messy."

"You think I don't know that?" he growled.

J.T. held his stare, refusing to back down. "Sometimes you can do all the right things and still get a bad outcome."

To his shame, Wolf felt the pinprick of tears behind his eyelids. He hated this feeling of helplessness. So he lashed out. "Speaking from experience, J.T.?"

The guy didn't even flinch. "Yeah, I am."

Wolf lowered his gaze, swallowed several times then forced a note of calm in his voice. "I'll take what you've said under advisement."

"Meaning you didn't hear a word I said."

"I heard you." Wolf rose.

J.T. followed suit. "You still want to go to lunch?"

No. But he was no coward. He met J.T.'s gaze and grinned. "As long as we can talk about football."

Scooting around his desk, J.T. gripped Wolf's shoulder. "I think that can be arranged. You a University of Georgia fan?"

Wolf thought about Hailey's over-the-top reaction at the silent auction. She'd been a little rabid—but kind of cute, too—when she'd lost out on her bid to spend a day with the school's mascot. "I'm becoming one."

"Good man."

They headed for the door, but Wolf stopped midway, remembering the initial reason for his visit. "Before we go, I need a list of Savannah's homeless shelters and food banks."

J.T. looked at him oddly. "Why?"

"I want to take Hailey on a date before she leaves for Haiti."

"To a homeless shelter?"

"You got a problem with that?"

For a moment, J.T. just stared at him. Then he released a quick laugh. "Not at all." He went back to his computer. Fingers on the keyboard, he asked, "You need phone numbers and addresses, too?"

"If you have them."

"Give me a sec." He moved his mouse around, left-clicked a few times, then typed something on the keyboard. The next thing Wolf heard was the sound of a printer firing up.

J.T grinned. "You're in business, soldier."

Finally, Wolf thought, something was going his way.

At precisely 0900 Wednesday morning, Hailey locked her front door. She turned and caught sight of Wolf coming up her walkway.

She studied him as he approached. He was dressed

in what she was coming to recognize as his civilian uniform. Worn jeans that hung low on his lean hips, a black T-shirt that clung to his muscular chest and a leather jacket that topped off the masculine ensemble rather nicely. The guy was a walking magazine ad for an expensive men's cologne.

Her stomach quivered in reaction.

The Lord had brought Wolf into her life at the worst possible time, under the worst possible circumstances. And yet, she couldn't help but feel blessed he was here with her now.

Of course, she'd be foolish to forget he'd initially sought her out because her brother had asked him to find her. The reality, always in the back of her mind, left Hailey feeling a bit depressed.

Still, she headed down her front steps with a light heart. Drawing closer to him, she caught a whiff of spice and soap that was pure Wolf.

She smiled. "Good morning."

"Good morning." He dropped his gaze and grinned back. "I see you dressed comfortably." His smile broadened. "I always did like a woman who could follow orders."

She tried not to smile at his teasing manner. "Yeah, well, don't get used to it."

"Wouldn't dream of it." Still smiling, he pulled her arm through his and steered her toward the heart of downtown.

The sensation of being this near to him, walking arm in arm like a real couple, was incredibly appealing. Hailey found herself snuggling closer. Wolf's grip tightened, just a little, enough to communicate he was enjoying this, as well.

When they passed by his car, Hailey realized she

had no idea where they were going. "We aren't taking Stella?"

"Nope. We're walking."

Determined to go with the flow and be flexible, Hailey held silent for two entire city blocks. But curiosity got the best of her midway down the third street. "Where are you taking me?"

He laughed. "I knew you wouldn't last the whole way without asking."

Was she that predictable? Or did he just know her that well? "So…?"

"We're going to the Savannah People's Mission, your town's version of a soup kitchen." He slanted a challenging look at her. "You've heard of it, right?"

"Sure I have."

Which was mostly true. Months ago, J.T. had given her a list of all the homeless shelters, soup kitchens and food banks in town. She'd read about the organizations then shoved the paper in the back of her Bible. Not because she was heartless, she told herself quickly, but because she wasn't involved with any of the ministries that would put her in a position to need their names and locations.

But now Wolf was taking her to a soup kitchen, within walking distance of her home. And, despite all her charity work in town, she'd never technically heard of it.

What did that say about her?

They rounded the corner of one of her favorite squares. A tiny grove of camellia bushes ran along the main sidewalk. Such pretty, bold flowers, daring to bloom when others lay dormant. The winter chill couldn't keep them down.

So engrossed with their courageous beauty, it took a

moment for Hailey to realize Wolf had stopped walking. She turned her head and gaped at all the people.

An impossibly long line snaked around a rectangular, nondescript building that stood adjacent to one of the historic churches open for daily tours. However, these people were not tourists. Some were dressed nicer than others, but they all had a look of defeat about them.

How had she driven by this building countless times in her life, but had never known it was a soup kitchen? "This is the Savannah People's Mission?"

Wolf hooked his thumbs through his belt loops. "You've never been here before?"

"No." And yet the mission was only a handful of blocks from her home.

Why hadn't she known it was so close? Why hadn't she *cared* enough to know?

She drew in a shaky breath.

"Let's go inside," Wolf suggested. "There's a lot to do before they open the doors for lunch."

A sudden wave of fear danced a chill up Hailey's spine and she remained frozen in place, unable to move. What if she couldn't help these people? What if they didn't accept her help?

"Come on." Wolf tugged her toward a side door. "We go in this way."

"You've been here before?"

"I came yesterday during my lunch hour."

"You did? Why?"

He lifted a shoulder. "I wanted to check it out before I brought you here."

He'd put a lot of forethought into this outing.

Gaze still locked with hers, Wolf drew her through the doorway.

The moment they stepped inside the building, a large

black woman gave a whoop and yanked Wolf into a bear hug. "Two days in a row." She pulled back and beamed at him. "What a blessing you are, my boy."

Wolf shrugged. "I can't seem to stay away." He slapped his palm onto his chest. "You've captured my heart, Cora Belle."

Giggling like a young girl, the large woman waved her spoon at him then caught sight of Hailey. "And who's this pretty thing?"

"I brought you another helper. Hailey O'Brien, meet Cora Belle, the best cook in Savannah."

Laughing at Wolf's outrageous compliment, the big lady smiled at Hailey. "Any friend of this boy's is welcome in my kitchen. Besides—" she jabbed Wolf with her elbow "—I'd never send away a helping hand."

Hailey instantly liked Cora Belle, but she wasn't sure how to proceed. "I'm here to work," she offered, hoping she sounded more confident than she felt. "Just tell me what to do."

"I got plenty of hands in here." Cora Belle turned back to her stove. "Why don't you help Captain Ty and my husband set up tables in the dining room?"

That sounded like something she could do. Hailey might not be able to cook, but she could set a table with her eyes closed.

An hour later the dining hall was full of chattering people, hovering over full plates of food. Hailey had been assigned to the relatively simple task of serving the potatoes, but she still felt uncomfortable, much as Wolf had looked at the country club.

She didn't make eye contact with the people she served. She simply heaped a spoonful of potatoes on the empty plates thrust in front of her.

That made her a coward, she knew. But as much as

she disliked this new insight into her character, Hailey couldn't muster the courage to lift her head.

How could she serve the Lord, when she couldn't even look His people in the eye?

Please, dear God, give me the courage....

Gulping down her trepidation, she lifted her head and connected her gaze with a woman who looked to be her same age. Something about her felt familiar, yet Hailey was sure she didn't know her.

Perhaps it was the loneliness masked behind the woman's shaky smile. Over the last six months, Hailey had experienced that emotion far too often. Maybe that was the way to go. Strike common ground, connect on a personal level.

Hailey returned the smile.

The young woman looked quickly away and moved on.

So much for making eye contact, Hailey thought.

Feeling completely out of her element, she caught sight of Wolf weaving his way from table to table.

Unlike her, he looked comfortable. He spoke to every person he came across, treating each one like a long-lost friend. He wasn't afraid to touch them, either. He clutched a few men on the shoulder, then placed a gentle hand under an elderly woman's elbow as he steered her to a seat at a table. For a man who'd experienced such an unsafe, lonely childhood, Wolf made family wherever he went. Not friends, *family*.

Hailey wondered if he realized that about himself.

Watching him work the room, she felt embarrassed by all the lofty speeches she'd given him about what it meant to serve people in need. Just like she'd always feared, she *was* a fraud.

Wolf, on the other hand, was authentic. And so at ease

with everyone he met. They gravitated toward him. He was probably just as good with his soldiers as he was with the people here today. Well, of course he was. Clay had said as much in his e-mails.

Hailey hadn't realized she'd been standing there, staring at him, until a kind-faced, middle-aged woman slid in beside her. "I'll take over if you need a break. You've been serving for a full hour."

"I have?"

The woman gently pulled the spoon out of Hailey's hand. "Go on, get yourself a plate and join the others."

"Oh, I couldn't possibly take food."

"Volunteers are encouraged to eat with our guests." She bumped hips with Hailey. "Go on. Make some friends."

"Sure. I can do that." Hailey drew her lip between her teeth and moved to the back of the line.

Once she had a full plate of food, she chose a seat at a table where the young woman she'd made eye contact with earlier sat.

"Hi."

No response.

Hailey tried not to sigh. "I'm Hailey."

Still no response.

"Mind if I sit with you?"

The woman raked her with blunt appraisal. "It's a free country."

Find that common ground, Hailey told herself. *Don't give up.* "Like I said, I'm Hailey." She spoke softly. "What's your name?"

"Sara."

"Really?" Hailey filled her fork with potatoes and

quickly took the bite. "My mother almost named me that."

"Why didn't she?"

"You know what?" Hailey let out a short little laugh. "I don't know."

Sara gave her a small smile, one that still had suspicion clinging to the edges.

"Do you have any kids?" Sara asked.

Unsure where this was going, Hailey shook her head. "No. I'm not married."

Sara tossed her fork down and snorted. "Like that matters."

Caught off guard by the woman's response, Hailey lowered her own fork. Less than five minutes into the conversation and she'd already managed to offend Sara.

Nevertheless, Hailey would not turn tail and run. Yet. "Do you have any children?" she asked.

An echo of a smile crossed her lips. "I have an eight-year-old daughter."

So old? Hailey did a quick calculation in her head. Unless she looked younger than she was, Sara had to have had the child when she was still a teenager.

"My daughter's in foster care right now," Sara explained. "It's been a tough year."

The shame in her eyes made it clear she did not like accepting charity.

"You don't have any family?" Hailey asked.

Sara lowered her head. "My parents disowned me when they found out I was pregnant."

Such a harsh response. If only Hailey knew what to do to help her. She didn't think money was the answer. Sara needed a long-term solution.

Hailey remembered a story in Scripture where the

disciples didn't give alms to a blind man but gave him his sight instead.

What would be the equivalent here? A job, maybe?

She had all kinds of contacts in the business community. Surely one of them would hire Sara.

Unable to make any guarantees, *yet,* Hailey stayed focused on their conversation. "What's your daughter's name?"

"Sara." She gave a self-deprecating shrug. "I never did have much imagination."

Hailey reached to her, touching her sleeve with a tentative hand. "Why not name your daughter after yourself? Men do it all the time. My brother was named after my father."

"Was?"

"He died in Iraq," Hailey said. "Six months ago."

Sara's shoulders slumped forward. "I lost my boyfriend, Tyler, back in the early months of the war. He was called up before we could get married. We were waiting until he came home." Her voice filled with regret. "But he never came home."

How awful. "How'd your boyfriend die?"

Sara's lips trembled. "His Humvee hit an IED."

A gasp flew out of Hailey before she could stop it. "I'm so sorry."

I want to live with them, cry with them, find joy and hope with them. Had Hailey really said those words to Wolf only a few nights ago? She'd been referring to people of other cultures, like the ones she would meet in Haiti next week. But here, right in front of her, God had given her someone who needed her help now. Not next week. *Now.*

"My brother died from an IED, too," she said.

A look of unity passed between her and Sara. Tragedy

had struck them both, but Hailey had had money and security to soften the blow of her loss.

Sara had not been so fortunate. She'd been disowned by her family, unmarried and completely on her own. Without the official help of the military she'd been left destitute.

Hailey would help her. She just had to figure out how.

Chapter Fifteen

Wolf watched Hailey scribble on a piece of paper then hand it to the woman she'd been speaking with since sitting down. With their heads bent close together, they looked as if they were in the middle of a serious conversation.

Once again, Hailey had surprised him. She'd clearly been uncomfortable when they'd first arrived, but that hadn't stopped her from helping where she was needed. She'd moved tables, stacked plates, served food and now was in the process of doing what she did best. Impacting another person's life for the better.

"You look at that gal the way my husband used to look at me when we were first married," Cora Belle said with a dreamy glint in her eyes.

Completely unconcerned he'd been busted for staring at Hailey, Wolf laughed. "He doesn't look at you like that anymore?"

"It's different now." But as soon as she made her claim, Cora Belle waggled her fingers at her husband. He paused in the middle of wiping a table and tossed her a wink.

"It doesn't look so different to me. In fact," Wolf said,

grinning, "that light is burning so strong I might have to put my sunglasses back on."

She slapped him lightly on the arm. "Oh, you."

Wolf relaxed against the wall behind him. "How long have you two been married, Cora Belle?"

"Fifty-three years come next March."

Talk about staying power. Wolf was impressed. "What's your secret?"

Before answering, the older woman smiled after her husband as he walked back into the kitchen, arms full of dirty plates. "Having the Lord in our lives is the key." She pursed her lips. "But it also helps to like the person you're married to. Makes everything else go easier."

Wolf looked over at Hailey again. She was still deep in her conversation. As he watched her, a solid sense of peace spread through him. The emotion settled over him like a whisper.

Yeah, he liked Hailey. No question about it. But his feelings were far more complicated than simple "like." And more significant. If she walked away from him now, if she were hurt or killed, Wolf wasn't sure he'd ever get over losing her.

His fingers curled together, every muscle in his body growing tense as the truth washed over him.

He didn't just like Hailey. He loved her.

She was strong and sweet and the best person he'd ever met. She'd brought him back to life, and then made him desire an existence beyond himself, beyond just going through the motions of the day.

But was he meant to be with her? Could he provide for her and give her the family she deserved? There were a lot of obstacles standing between them—their different pasts, their conflicting goals for the future and the largest obstacle of all, Clay.

There was suddenly too much to think about, too many questions without answers.

Wolf crossed his arms over his chest and cleared his mind.

Eyeing him like a dog on point, Cora Belle wiped her hands on her food-stained apron, slowly, methodically. Then her gaze narrowed even more. "You gonna marry that girl?"

"That was direct."

"Then give me an equally direct answer."

Wolf shut his eyes a moment. The question should have shocked him, should have sent warning bells clanging in his head. Instead, he felt nothing but confusion, mixed with equal parts hope and fear. "I...don't know."

Cora Belle shook her head at him, disappointment pulling her lips into a frown. "Don't take too long to figure it out." She nodded toward Hailey. "That one isn't going to sit on the shelf for long."

Wolf's breath clogged in his throat. Cora Belle spoke the truth. Hailey wouldn't stay single for long. She was meant to have a family, with a husband who treasured her and put her first in his life.

Wolf wanted to be that man. He wanted to be Hailey's family. But could he give her what she deserved? Did he have what it took to make her happy?

Did he even have the right to try?

Wolf was silent on the walk back to Hailey's house. She hadn't noticed at first, probably because she'd been too busy thinking about Sara.

Hailey was in a unique position to help her new friend. Before today, she'd looked at her charity work—especially sitting on all those boards—as a hindrance to her service for the Lord. But she now realized all those years of making contacts in the business community were invaluable.

Hailey had the tools to help Sara. She also had her own personal experience to better help her understand the woman's loss.

All this time she'd been setting her sights on ministry halfway across the world, which she still firmly believed was her calling, but maybe the Lord was showing her another way to serve in the meantime. *Maybe* it wasn't a matter of all or nothing, but a matter of serving in more than one capacity.

"I understand why you took me to the Mission," she said to Wolf as she unlocked her front door.

He followed her inside, a frown digging a groove across his forehead. "Why's that?"

"You wanted to show me there are people in need right here in my own city, people I'm uniquely qualified to help."

He frowned. "I wasn't trying to manipulate you."

"Sure you were," she said without an ounce of resentment. "But I don't hold it against you. I can be stubborn. The only way to tell me about the need was to *show* me."

"So you aren't upset with me?"

"No." She waited for him to close the front door then slipped her hands up his arms, clasped them behind his neck. "In fact, I want to thank you." She lifted on her toes. "Thank you, Wolf."

Before she connected her lips to his, he lowered his head and did the deed himself.

She sighed against him.

After a few moments, he lifted his head and stared

intently in her eyes. "Does this mean you won't be going to the Middle East?"

"No." She blew out a frustrated breath and stepped out of his embrace. "It means I'm willing to serve in Savannah *and* the Middle East. I can do both."

He didn't argue with her, but simply stared at her. And stared. And stared. "Fair enough."

His words sounded so...final. Like he was saying goodbye to her. "You aren't going to fight me on this?"

"Hailey, when I first arrived on your doorstep, I expected to meet a teenager, a girl with one foot in adulthood and the other still in childhood. I expected my task to be easy. A quick conversation and my duty to Clay would be complete."

His duty to Clay. The only reason he'd sought her out. She'd thought they'd come so far from that day, that they'd managed to build a relationship that was solely theirs. But now she wasn't so sure. More frightening still, if Wolf failed to convince her to stay home, if he stopped fighting her about the Middle East, would he walk away for good?

"I was wrong about you on so many levels," he continued. "You're a beautiful, independent woman, capable of taking care of yourself."

Was he letting her go? "Thanks."

He pressed his fingertips to the bridge of his nose. "I'm not trying to insult you." He dropped his hand and looked directly at her. "I'm trying to tell you I think you're wonderful, beautiful, talented and gifted."

If he thought all those things about her, then why did he sound so grim?

"But when it's all said and done," he continued, "I—"

"Still see me as Clay's little sister." The realization ripped at her heart.

"I don't know, Hailey. I don't know where my feelings of guilt and duty end and where my love for you begins. All I know is that I *will* protect you, even if that means going to the Middle East with you."

"Did you just say you love me?" she whispered.

"Yes, I love you." He practically growled the words.

She'd never expected to hear such a sad, pitiful declaration. Not from Wolf.

Didn't he know he was breaking her heart?

She had to ask him the hard question, the one they'd been dancing around for weeks. "But do you love me because I'm me or because I'm Clay's little sister?"

He didn't answer her. Pushing past her, he walked into the kitchen and pulled the picture of her and Clay off the refrigerator.

"He didn't deserve to die," he said in such a low voice she barely caught his words.

"No, he didn't." She stared at the picture, her stomach wrenching over their mutual loss. "But he did die, and now we have to go on. Life is all about loss, Wolf. We either let it cripple us or let it make us stronger."

He didn't respond, but just kept staring at the picture. "Would he approve of us being together?"

Hailey knew the answer, knew it as sure as she knew her own name. "Haven't you ever wondered why he told me so much about you?"

He continued staring at the photograph. "Because we worked closely together. I was always on his mind."

"It was more than that." She touched his arm, certainty filling her. "Clay wanted us to be together."

"No." Wolf shook his head vigorously. "He didn't

want any man to have you, especially not a man like me, who knows nothing about family."

"Of course you know. I watched you at the soup kitchen today. You made those people feel comfortable and at home, like they belonged to a large, happy family. I also saw how Cora Belle treated you like her own son, and she's only known you for two days."

He was silent for a long moment, his gaze still glued to the picture in his hand. "You're embellishing the facts."

"I'm speaking the truth. I've seen you in action. You understand family better than most men I know."

"Even if what you say is accurate—" he turned the picture around his palm "—you know where I come from, what my childhood was like. Clay wouldn't have wanted you with someone like me."

"That's just absurd. Clay was never a judgmental jerk." She raised her voice to make her point. "How dare you suggest otherwise."

He snapped his gaze in her direction and the picture dropped to the floor.

Finally, Hailey had his complete attention. "Now you listen to me, Captain Wolfson. Your childhood never mattered to my brother. And it doesn't matter to me."

He blinked at her, his shock evident in his eyes.

Softening her expression, Hailey cupped his face tenderly. "Oh, Wolf, don't you understand? I'm only concerned with your future, and whether or not you have room for me in it."

Sighing heavily, he relaxed into her palm, then reared back.

She let her hand drop to her side, saddened by the internal struggle she saw on his face.

"Hailey, don't look at me like that. I can't think with

you touching me. And I *need* to think. It would be too easy to ignore my doubts, to go with my feelings rather than the facts, but that wouldn't be fair to you."

Maybe he was right, but she was afraid to let him walk out of her home with their conversation unresolved, especially knowing that next week she'd be leaving for Haiti.

Trust the Lord. He's already got this worked out. The thought came to her with such clarity she felt a huge sense of relief flow through her. If she and Wolf were meant to be together, God would make that happen.

She also had to trust that Wolf truly loved her, for her, not out of misguided guilt or loyalty to a fallen friend. That he would ultimately see her as his family and his future.

In the meantime, it couldn't hurt to give him a little nudge in the right direction.

"Wait right here. I have something for you." She turned to go then swung back around. "Don't leave."

"I won't."

She ran to her room, dug the box of Clay's e-mails out from under her bed and then rushed back into the kitchen.

"These are the e-mails Clay sent me from Iraq." She held out the box to Wolf. "I printed them out."

He raised his hands in the air, palms facing forward. "They're private, between you and your brother."

"Please, Wolf, I want you to read them, especially the ones concerning you."

His hands dropped to his sides and a look of confusion blanketed his face. "Why?"

"You'll understand once you do." She pressed her lips to his cheek. "Take your time reading them. I leave for

Haiti next week. I think it's best we don't see each other until I get back. We can talk more then."

He didn't argue, which made her think about despairing, but she didn't give in to the emotion. She was going to trust God all the way.

Putting on a brave face, she walked Wolf to the door. "I love you."

Without another word, she kissed him on the lips, gave him a shaky smile then shut the door in his face.

Chapter Sixteen

Ten days, seven hours and twelve minutes after Hailey kicked Wolf out of her home, he paced through his town house.

His steps were jerky and out of sync, not so much because his leg ached but because his heart ached. He shouldn't have honored Hailey's demand to stay away from her until after she returned from Haiti. He shouldn't have let her leave the country with so much unsettled between them.

What if she got hurt while she was away? What if she were kidnapped? The muscles around his heart clenched in helpless agony.

What if she didn't come back at all?

Gritting his teeth, Wolf prowled into the living room and turned on the television. A twenty-four-hour weather report popped onto the screen. For the last six days, Wolf had alternated between this station and various news channels. If anything disastrous happened in Haiti, he would know as soon as it occurred.

Unfortunately, having immediate access to vast amounts of information only made him feel more uneasy, not less.

This was what came from caring. This dark sense of foreboding. This inability to calm down as he waited anxiously for news from the troubled region.

Though military husbands and wives had to cope with this every day, it took a great amount of courage and love. And wasn't that the bottom line? Wolf loved Hailey enough to suffer through these moments of fear and helplessness.

So what was holding him back from committing his future to hers? His promise to Clay? His brutal childhood? Maybe a combination of both?

He thought back over his last conversation with Hailey. She'd claimed she didn't care where Wolf came from, and had scolded him for suggesting that Clay might have held his past against him.

Wolf smiled at the memory of her fierce reaction. Hailey was quite the little warrior in her own right.

And now, when it might be too late, Wolf realized he wanted to spend the rest of his life with Hailey O'Brien. He wanted to build a family with her, to serve beside her, to grow old with her.

But did he deserve her? Could he make her happy?

Perhaps the answer was in Clay's e-mails, as Hailey had claimed. Wolf glanced over at the box she had given him. It sat on the coffee table, in the same spot he'd left it ten days ago.

The time had come to read Clay's words to his sister.

With a mixture of impatience and dread, Wolf sat on his couch and placed the box on his lap.

Keeping his emotions in check, he took a deep breath and pulled off the lid. Retrieving the large stack of papers, he tossed the box aside and read the first e-mail. Then he read the next one. And the next.

By the fourth, grief clogged in his throat.

Clay was all over these e-mails. His sense of humor and love of life jumped off the pages. The pain that came from remembering his friend was almost too much for Wolf, like someone had slammed a dagger in his gut and twisted.

Releasing a hiss, he leaned his head back against the sofa. A shudder slipped down his spine. Though he didn't want to continue, he had to keep reading. For Hailey. And maybe for his own sake, as well.

He grabbed another page, skimmed the e-mail until he came to Clay's suggestion for Hailey to think bigger than her current charity work.

"There are people all over the world who need the love of Christ," Wolf read aloud. "You could be the one to carry that hope beyond Savannah, Hailey. With your faith in God and your gift with people, you could make a difference in the Middle East. More than I can as a soldier."

Breathing hard, Wolf crushed the paper in his hand. Hailey hadn't misunderstood her brother after all. Clay had encouraged her to go into ministry. In the Middle East.

No wonder she'd been so filled with conviction.

Wolf squeezed his eyes shut and forced his mind back to that fateful day on the Iraqi roadside.

He would never forget his friend's last words. "No...mission work," Clay had said. "Not here. Not by herself."

Not by herself. Clay's change of heart had been about Hailey's safety. He'd wanted to guarantee his sister didn't put herself into unnecessary danger.

Wolf would never let that happen.

If the Lord called Hailey to the Middle East, he wouldn't stop her. He would go with her.

But would Clay approve?

At this point, there was only one way to find out.

Wolf swallowed and read the next e-mail. There was a lot of nothing in this one, mainly gripes about the dry desert heat and having to fill out situation reports that were long overdue.

Wolf chuckled. Clay had always been behind on his paperwork.

Still smiling, Wolf returned his attention to his friend's words. He read his name and everything in him froze.

Wolf is the brother I never had and the best man I know. When you meet him, you'll think so, too.

Wolf flipped through the stack until he found another one about him. *Wolf saved a child today. He jumped in front of a fast-moving car and whipped the kid into his arms. He never hesitated. He'll make a great father. When you meet him, I know you'll agree.*

Wolf read three more e-mails. And then another five. In all the ones where Clay mentioned his name four words showed up, as well.

When you meet him...

Clay had been matchmaking. Almost as if he'd known he wouldn't get the opportunity to introduce them to each other himself. Had he sensed his imminent death?

Wolf's breath hitched in his throat. No matter how many of Clay's e-mails he read, guilt still held its nasty grip on him. Would regret always rule him?

Somehow Wolf had to find a way to surrender this to the Lord. He went in search of his Bible. Something he should have done months ago, but had been too angry at God to bother.

After nearly an hour of searching, he found the weathered book at the bottom of a box he'd yet to unpack.

Hands shaking, he sat back down on the sofa and flipped through the pages at random. He read aloud the first Scripture that caught his eye, one in the book of Acts. "Everyone who believes in Him receives forgiveness of sins through His name."

Wolf looked up to heaven. "Is it really that easy, Lord? Do I simply believe and this terrible feeling goes away?"

If that were true, healing would have already come. He turned a few pages to his left. Still in Acts, he read, "Repent then, and turn to God, so that your sins may be wiped out."

Believe. Repent. There had to be more to it than that.

Wolf flipped the pages in the opposite direction, stopping in First John this time. "This is love; not that we loved God, but that He loved us and sent His Son as an atoning sacrifice for our sins."

Finally, Wolf knew what he had to do to move past his guilt. He had to believe. Repent. And then receive the gift that had already been given to him.

He lowered himself to his knees and buried his face in his hands.

"Lord, thank You for covering my sins with Your sacrifice. Help me to receive Your forgiveness so I can forgive myself."

Lowering his hands, Wolf took a deep breath. A sense of peace spread through him.

Although he knew God still had a lot of work to do in him, Wolf rose to his feet. Smiling.

* * *

Hailey headed toward baggage claim, exhausted, filthy and emotionally wrung out. She'd rushed off the plane ahead of her fellow team members, determined to get to Wolf's town house as quickly as possible.

Despite this sense of urgency, there was joy in her heart, too.

She had gone to Port-Au-Prince determined to make at least one personal connection. She'd made several.

Her time in the Haiti slum had changed her. The people at the Savannah People's Mission had changed her.

Wolf had changed her.

She had so much to tell him about her trip, about the children she'd met. And the old man who'd accepted Christ right before he'd succumbed to cancer. But first...

Hailey just wanted to see Wolf, tell him she loved him and have him hold her in his strong arms for a while.

She wanted to be with him, always. No more obstacles. No more uneasiness between them. Just together. They'd work out the rest of the details as they went along.

Eager to get to him, Hailey picked up the pace but stopped in her tracks when she saw his familiar form several yards on the other side of security.

Wolf had come to the airport to meet her.

Relief, joy, pleasure, all three rushed through her, making her heart stutter in her chest.

Since Wolf hadn't noticed her yet, she drank in the sight of him. He wore black pants, a plain white T-shirt and his trademark leather jacket. He looked good. Really good.

He was standing next to J.T., completely caught up in

their conversation. They were both broad-shouldered, lean, handsome men. Hard men with soft hearts—not that either one of them would admit to that last part.

Wolf looked up at last. The moment he caught sight of her, a smile spread across his lips. It was his wolf smile.

Hailey's blood thickened in her veins. Wolf was her man. Her future. Her bold warrior. Hers. Hers. Hers!

So what was she doing standing here staring at him? He gave her a look that asked the same question.

She dropped her carry-on and set out at a dead run. On something between a sob and a laugh, she launched herself into his arms.

He caught her hard against his chest, then buried his face in her hair. "Welcome home, sweetheart."

"Oh, Wolf, I missed you."

"Yeah. Me, too."

They clung to each other, ignoring everyone around them, pretending it didn't matter that the last time they'd seen each other Hailey had kicked him out of her house.

She pulled back, went in for a kiss but froze when J.T. cleared his throat.

Far less embarrassed than she should be, Hailey stepped away from Wolf. But she kept her hand on his arm, half-afraid he might disappear if she gave him the chance. "Hi, J.T. I...I didn't mean to ignore you."

"Sure you did." His eyes gleamed with amusement. "But no offense taken. You had other..." He gave her a knowing grin. "Priorities on your mind."

She let out a little laugh, glancing at Wolf sideways. Their eyes locked and they shared a brief moment of homecoming.

Wolf moved behind her, wrapped his arms around her waist then rested his chin on her head.

Still grinning, J.T. lifted his eyebrows. "Okay. I see you two have a lot of catching up to do. And I have the rest of my team to welcome home."

Wolf pulled Hailey tighter against him. "You're not intruding, J.T." His voice said differently.

"You're not," Hailey agreed halfheartedly. "We just haven't seen each other in a while and we... Oh, my carry-on. I left it..." She shot out of Wolf's arms and looked helplessly around her. "Somewhere."

J.T. chuckled. "It's over there, on this side of security. I'll bring it down to baggage claim for you." He turned in the direction Hailey had just come. "I'll meet you two downstairs in a few minutes."

"Thanks, J.T.," she called after him.

He tossed a wave over his head. "My pleasure."

An uncomfortable silence fell in his wake.

Now that Hailey was alone with Wolf, and the initial pleasure of seeing him had worn off, she felt a flood of uncharacteristic shyness wash over her. Sighing, she twisted her hands together.

When five long seconds passed and Wolf didn't speak, either, she lifted her gaze to his. Relieved at what she saw in his eyes, she relaxed. Wolf loved her. He wanted to be with her.

Everything was going to work out just fine.

Tugging her gently toward him, Wolf lowered his forehead to hers. She clutched at his arms.

"Let's get the rest of your luggage. And then we'll head home." He stepped back and caressed her cheek. "I have a lot to tell to you."

"Oh, Wolf. Me, too." She tipped her face up to his. "I lo—"

"Not here." He pressed his finger tenderly to her lips. "Let's wait until it's just the two of us."

Just the two of us. She liked the sound of that.

A lot.

Chapter Seventeen

Hailey entered her living room with anxious excitement nearly busting out of her. She was home. Wolf was here with her. The rest would work itself out in time.

She moved through the room, turning on lights while Wolf set her bags at the bottom of the stairs.

Once he joined her again, she went to him and wrapped her arms around his waist.

Feeling at peace, she smiled up at him. He was her big, handsome warrior. His blue, blue eyes were filled with genuine tenderness, the kind of look every woman dreamed she'd see in the eyes of the man she loved. "I'm glad you came to the airport to pick me up. I—"

"You're different."

"I am?"

He hesitated, just a little, then ran his hand down her hair, hooking a tendril around his finger. "I mean that in a good way."

There was affection in his eyes, and a deeper emotion. *Love.* He was through fighting the inevitable, through fighting the notion of them being together.

Hailey's stomach fluttered in anticipation of the future that lay ahead of them. But first, they had to deal with the obstacles that still stood in their way. "You look different, too." She angled her head. "More at peace."

"I am. I…" He stepped away from her, giving her the opportunity to read his expression as he spoke. "I'm not drowning in guilt anymore."

She could see the truth of his words, in the way his gaze held hers without faltering, in the way his shoulders remained straight and unflinching.

"Oh, Wolf, you've forgiven yourself." Tears of joy welled in her eyes.

"I don't know if I'd go that far." He ran a hand through his hair. "But I've given it up to God."

She wiped at her cheeks and sighed. "That's the first step."

"I'll always regret what happened to my men." The slight catch in his voice revealed his continued grief. "But I'm done questioning things I can't change. I can't keep looking backward." He shut his eyes a moment, then shook his head and reopened them. "I have to start looking forward."

He was so courageous, so strong. Was there any wonder she was in love with him?

With another sigh she moved forward, and placed her palm on his chest, near his heart.

He covered her hand with his, but didn't speak again. He didn't have to. His eyes said everything. He was right here with her. In the moment. Present and awake. Ready for whatever came next. "Looking forward," she whispered. "I like the sound of that."

He smiled at last. "Tell me about your trip."

She'd give him the details later. For now she wanted to focus on the lesson she'd learned. "I discovered something very important while I was gone."

He lifted an eyebrow.

"I learned that there are hurting people everywhere, people who need compassion and grace, understanding and mercy. The things I can give them as a servant of Christ."

His hand dropped away from hers. "What are you saying, Hailey?"

"I'm saying..." She let her own hand flutter to her side. "That I don't have to go to the Middle East to do the Lord's work."

"Does that mean you're not going to pursue a posting overseas?" His voice remained neutral, as did his gaze. The only clue to his thoughts came in the slight tightening of his jaw.

Grateful for his subdued reaction, she answered him frankly. "No. It means I'm not going to serve the Lord with blinders on anymore. I'm going to go where He sends me, whether that turns out to be here in Savannah, or a Caribbean island, or the Middle East."

Wolf frowned faintly, shaking his head. "Is this change of heart because of me?"

"Not *because* of you, no. But you did play a role in my decision. You helped me see past my grief over Clay's death to the truth. I don't have to go to the Middle East to honor my brother's life." She walked over to the sofa, then perched a hip on the arm. "I can do that anywhere."

Nodding, he shifted to face her head-on. "I want you to know that *if* you're called to the Middle East," he said, "you won't go alone."

She instantly understood his meaning and loved him all the more for it. "And who, might I ask, would go with me?"

"Someone who knows the region and the culture." He stepped closer, staring at her with a serious expression on his face. "Someone who understands the enemy, as well as the locals."

"Someone like…oh, say, a United States Army captain?"

He smiled at last. "That would be the ideal choice."

What a generous, selfless man he was. Hailey had found something richer and stronger with Wolf than she'd ever dreamed possible. "But that would mean quitting the Army." She grimaced as the realization sank in. "I would never ask you to sacrifice your future for me."

"*You're* my future, Hailey." He moved closer still, close enough to reach down and cup her cheek. "God has a plan for both of us, together. We'll make our own family, always looking ahead of us and not behind. That might involve me quitting the Army, or it might not."

She closed her eyes a moment and leaned into his hand. "You're sure this is what you want, Wolf? Are you sure you want me? Us? No more worries over whether or not Clay would approve?"

"I read his e-mails." Wolf dropped his hand. "He wanted us together."

She smiled and nodded.

"He also wanted you to go to the Middle East. As long as I keep you as safe as humanly possible, I will have fulfilled my duty."

"No more guilt over his death?"

"I'll always wish things had turned out differently, but I'm learning to accept that there are some things I can't control. Accidents happen."

Hailey had never been more proud of him than in that moment. He'd come so far. "Oh, Wolf, I love you."

"I love you, too, Hailey."

She rose, lifted onto her tiptoes, and then pressed her

lips to his in a fleeting kiss that left her mouth tingling when she pulled away.

"I still have a few years of active duty left." He placed his hands on her waist, but then let them drop just as quickly. "I will be deployed again in that time. After all you've been through, all your losses, waiting for me is a lot to ask of you."

She gave him a soft smile. "If there's anything I've learned in the past few years, it's to take whatever joy I can today because there might not be a tomorrow."

He kissed one of her hands and then the other. "You're amazing."

"I want to be with you, Wolf, however long that turns out to be."

"I may never leave the military," he warned.

She wouldn't ask it of him, ever. That was between him and the Heavenly Father. "We'll take each day as it comes."

"I'm thinking about going back to school part-time. I want to take a few seminary classes, see if that's where God is leading me."

"I'll support you, no matter what."

"Even if I become an Army chaplain? Despite what you might think, Hailey, it's a dangerous job, especially in wartime."

"Maybe I haven't made myself clear. I want to be with you, whatever that means, wherever it takes us. You are my family now, and I'm yours. We'll face the future together, as a unit."

"Even knowing our future is uncertain?" he asked, stepping back so he could stare into her eyes.

"No one's future is certain. Whether you're a soldier or a minister, whether I'm called to stay in Savannah or travel to the Middle East, I want us to serve the Lord together."

"So we go where God leads us?" he asked. "No personal agendas, no firm plans, just open minds and open hearts?"

"That sums it up nicely."

He lowered to one knee, and then smiled up at her. "Hailey O'Brien—" he took her hand and kissed her knuckles "—will you marry me?"

"Yes."

Laughing, he drew her into his arms and then lowered his mouth to hers. The kiss was slow, sweet and full of silent promises for their life together.

She couldn't have asked for a better homecoming.

Epilogue

One week later, Hailey's twenty-seventh birthday dawned windy and bone-chilling cold. The frigid air made Wolf's leg ache more than usual, but he was learning to accept the bad with the good. His leg fell under the bad column, but only when the air turned cold and wet.

Under the good column, Wolf had signed up for seminary classes yesterday and, today, he was going to make his engagement to Hailey official.

He'd been awake since 0400, but had decided to be a gentleman and wait until after sunrise to make the drive to Hailey's house.

A rush of joy surged through him as he drew Stella to a stop in the front of her home. All the lights were on.

Hailey was up…waiting for him.

Life was good.

The crate beside him shook, followed by a sad, pathetic whimper.

"Yeah, yeah. All right. You can come out now." Wolf opened the door to a face full of dog drool and crooked teeth.

Grinning down at Hailey's birthday gift, Wolf scratched the puppy's massive head.

"I must be in love," he muttered. "Why else would I buy an ugly mutt like you?"

The dog's sorry excuse for a tail started wagging.

"Hold still," Wolf said to the squirming bundle of bad breath and under-bite. "You're making it impossible to put this ribbon around your neck."

After more struggle, and a little unnecessary rough-housing, Wolf tied the bow. It hung at a cockeyed angle.

"You look ridiculous."

The miniature bulldog shook his head, sending the bow farther off-center.

"Hailey's going to love you."

In answer, the fat tongue went for his chin. Wolf dodged to his left and exited the car, puppy tucked under one arm.

He teetered up to Hailey's front door. "I think you've put on weight since we left the house."

The dog rolled his enormous eyes.

With his hands full, Wolf literally leaned on the door-bell. "Remember to smile."

Hailey swung open the door. "You're early." Her gaze dropped to the squirming puppy in his hands and she gasped. "Oh! Oh, Wolf! You didn't."

He smiled at her, a big loopy grin that probably matched the one on the ugly mutt's face. "Happy Birthday, sweetheart."

"I love him." She lifted misty eyes back to his face. "I love *you*."

"Now that's what I like to hear."

"Get in here." She tugged him forward.

Inside the living room, Wolf set the puppy on the carpet then straightened.

Hailey yanked him against her and kissed him hard on his lips. "Thank you, thank you, thank you."

"You're welcome."

After another kiss, longer and deeper than the first, Hailey dropped to her knees in front of the puppy. "What are we going to name him?" She raised her gaze up to Wolf. "It is a boy, right?"

"It's a boy." Wolf laughed. "To be honest, I'm partial to...Tank."

"Tank." She studied the dog with his broad shoulders, huge head and bowed legs. "I like it." She kissed the puppy on the head. "I dub thee Tank. The newest member of our family."

She and the dog wrestled on the floor for a while.

Wolf simply watched them. He was so happy to see Hailey falling in love with her new puppy he'd completely forgotten the other present he had for her. "Check Tank's bow."

Hailey cocked her head at him.

"Go on," he urged. "There's one more gift attached to the ribbon around his neck."

"Oh. *Oh!*" Reaching out, she began carefully untying the bow. She made it halfway through before her fingers froze.

Tears filled her eyes. "Oh, Wolf." She blinked at the engagement ring. "It's beautiful."

"Take it off the ribbon. Let's see if it fits." A wave of doubt filled him and his stomach rolled. "Unless you're having second thoughts about marrying me."

She twisted her lips at him, clearly insulted by the

mere suggestion. "No second thoughts. None whatsoever."

Her quick, heartfelt response loosened the knots in his gut.

She pulled the bow free and held up the ring he'd picked out. The simple square-cut diamond caught the light.

"It's gorgeous," she said.

The knots returned. He hadn't wanted to go too big, just shy of a carat, but maybe he hadn't gone big enough. "You're sure?"

"*Absolutely.*" She thrust it toward him. "Will you put it on me?"

He nodded, slowly. Emotion chocked the breath in his lungs. After two failed attempts, he managed to slide the ring on her finger.

"It's a perfect fit," she said, pressing her cheek to his.

"No, Hailey." He pulled her onto his lap and kissed her soundly on the mouth. "*You're* my perfect fit. In life and in love."

She snuggled deeper into his embrace. "Be careful, soldier. You're on the verge of getting a lifelong commitment out of me."

"That *was* the general idea behind the engagement ring. Ah, Hailey." He tightened his grip around her, "I want you in my life. Forever and always."

"Good thing you feel that way." She turned her face up to his. "Because you're never getting rid of me. Not in this lifetime."

A rush of love filled him.

After years of wandering from house to house, Army

post to Army post, Wolf was finally home. And ready to build a family with the beautiful, smart, talented woman of his dreams.

* * * * *

Be sure to pick up Renee Ryan's
next book, DANGEROUS ALLIES,
a thrilling historical set in World War II,
available in October 2010 only from
Love Inspired Historical.

Dear Reader,

Thank you for choosing *Homecoming Hero*. Writing this book was a special treat for me on so many levels. I have many military friends, both men and women, who have inspired me through the years with their commitment to their calling. It was a joy getting the opportunity to explore their daily lives. Any mistakes I made in writing this book are all mine.

I also enjoyed giving a none-too-subtle wink to my favorite spectator sport: college football. I love college football. And when I say I love it, I mean I love, love, love it! I'll watch just about any matchup on TV, but I especially like going to the games in person. There's something infectious about the game-day atmosphere. The crowds, the junk food, the noise, the band, the screaming/booing/cheering fans—all of these individual aspects mix together to form a sensory overload that leaves me pleasantly exhausted. I can't think of a better way to spend a Saturday.

Because of my husband's job, I've had the good fortune of living in many college towns over the years. I've attended games at some of the most famous stadiums in the country, as well as some of the not-so-famous ones. I've tailgated with die-hard boosters and people who want to talk about their hair rather than the game. I've sat in terrible seats, fabulous seats, skyboxes and even stood on the sidelines. I've memorized countless cheers and fight songs. I've watched the cheerleaders and the silly antics of the mascots. But there's one special mascot who has literally stolen my heart. I think you can figure out which one. He doesn't do much, except just be who he is. I love him for that. UGA, you're the man!

What about you? Any college football fans out there? Or would you rather talk hair? I'd love to hear your opinion on either. You can contact me at my Web site, www.reneeryan.com.

In the meantime, happy reading!

Renee

QUESTIONS FOR DISCUSSION

1. Why does Wolf seek out Hailey in the opening scene? What makes his task especially difficult? Is he right to try to stop her from her goal? Why or why not?

2. When Hailey discovers Wolf was the only survivor of the IED that killed her brother and three other soldiers, she realizes she has an opportunity to offer comfort to a wounded soul, yet she has no idea how to go about it. What does she do? Have you ever been in a position that stretched your capabilities? What did you do?

3. What is motivating Hailey's determination to become a missionary in the Middle East? Do you think she's naive, as Wolf claims? What's the difference between having a heart for causes versus having a heart for people?

4. What is Wolf's reaction to the missionaries' speech at Hailey's church? Why does he react that way? Do you think he overreacts? Why or why not?

5. Why do you think Wolf dislikes J.T. at first, despite their common backgrounds? What changes between the two that ultimately makes it possible for them to become friends? Have you ever had someone in your life who started out as an adversary but turned into a friend? What happened to make the change?

6. When Wolf asks Hailey to help him shop for items to put in his townhome, the excursion goes badly. What happens in the store? Why do you think Wolf reacts that way? What would you have done had you been Hailey?

7. Do you think Wolf's intense need for danger makes him an adrenaline junkie? What's really driving him to do the risky things he does? Do you agree with his assessment? Do you think God makes mistakes? Why or why not?

8. What does Wolf do to "shock" Hailey into staying home? Do you think it's unfair of him to show her those videos? Why do you think the exercise backfires on him?

9. When Hailey realizes she can't help Wolf overcome his guilt she turns to J.T. for help. What does he tell her? Why is his advice so hard for her to accept? Have you ever felt helpless in the face of a loved one's problem? What did you do?

10. What happens when Wolf takes Hailey to a homeless shelter that is mere blocks away from her house? Why do you think it's so hard for her to look people in the eye, at least at first? What changes in her as a direct result of her time with the homeless?

11. Why is Wolf afraid to love Hailey? What's holding him back? What happens when he reads her brother's e-mails from Iraq?

12. What happens to Hailey on her short-term mission trip to Haiti? Why is this change significant? Have you ever thought God was calling you to go in one direction, only to discover He had something else planned for your life? What happened?

Love Inspired

TITLES AVAILABLE NEXT MONTH

Available August 31, 2010

BABY MAKES A MATCH
Chatam House
Arlene James

DOCTOR RIGHT
Alaskan Bride Rush
Janet Tronstad

SHELTER OF HOPE
New Friends Street
Lyn Cote

LOVE FINDS A HOME
Mirror Lake
Kathryn Springer

MADE TO ORDER FAMILY
Ruth Logan Herne

COURTING RUTH
Hannah's Daughters
Emma Miller

LARGER-PRINT BOOKS!

**GET 2 FREE
LARGER-PRINT NOVELS
PLUS 2 FREE
MYSTERY GIFTS**

Larger-print novels are now available...

YES! Please send me 2 FREE LARGER-PRINT Love Inspired® novels and my 2 FREE mystery gifts (gifts are worth about $10). After receiving them, if I don't wish to receive any more books, I can return the shipping statement marked "cancel". If I don't cancel, I will receive 6 brand-new novels every month and be billed just $4.74 per book in the U.S. or $5.24 per book in Canada. That's a saving of over 20% off the cover price. It's quite a bargain! Shipping and handling is just 50¢ per book.* I understand that accepting the 2 free books and gifts places me under no obligation to buy anything. I can always return a shipment and cancel at any time. Even if I never buy another book, the two free books and gifts are mine to keep forever.

122/322 IDN E7QP

Name	(PLEASE PRINT)	

Address		Apt. #

City	State/Prov.	Zip/Postal Code

Signature (if under 18, a parent or guardian must sign)

Mail to Steeple Hill Reader Service:
IN U.S.A.: P.O. Box 1867, Buffalo, NY 14240-1867
IN CANADA: P.O. Box 609, Fort Erie, Ontario L2A 5X3

Not valid to current subscribers to Love Inspired Larger-Print books.

**Are you a current subscriber to Love Inspired books
and want to receive the larger-print edition?
Call 1-800-873-8635 or visit www.morefreebooks.com.**

* Terms and prices subject to change without notice. Prices do not include applicable taxes. Sales tax applicable in N.Y. Canadian residents will be charged applicable provincial taxes and GST. Offer not valid in Quebec. This offer is limited to one order per household. All orders subject to approval. Credit or debit balances in a customer's account(s) may be offset by any other outstanding balance owed by or to the customer. Please allow 4 to 6 weeks for delivery. Offer available while quantities last.

Your Privacy: Steeple Hill Books is committed to protecting your privacy. Our Privacy Policy is available online at www.SteepleHill.com or upon request from the Reader Service. From time to time we make our lists of customers available to reputable third parties who may have a product or service of interest to you. If you would prefer we not share your name and address, please check here. ☐

Help us get it right—We strive for accurate, respectful and relevant communications. To clarify or modify your communication preferences, visit us at www.ReaderService.com/consumerschoice.

LILPI0R

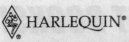

HARLEQUIN®

American ★ Romance®

TANYA MICHAELS
Texas Baby

Babies
&
Bachelors
USA

Instant parenthood is turning Addie Caine's life
upside down. Caring for her young nephew and
infant niece is rewarding—but exhausting! So when
a gorgeous man named Giff Baker starts a short-term
assignment at her office, Addie knows there's no time
for romance. Yet Giff seems to be in hot pursuit....
Is this part of his job, or can he really be falling
for her? And her chaotic, ready-made family!

**Available September 2010
wherever books are sold.**

"LOVE, HOME & HAPPINESS"

www.eHarlequin.com

HAR75325